BLOOD BORN

ALSO BY SHELLEY WILSON

The Last Princess
Hood Academy
The Phantom's Curse

THE GUARDIANS SERIES

Guardians of the Dead
Guardians of the Sky
Guardians of the Lost Lands

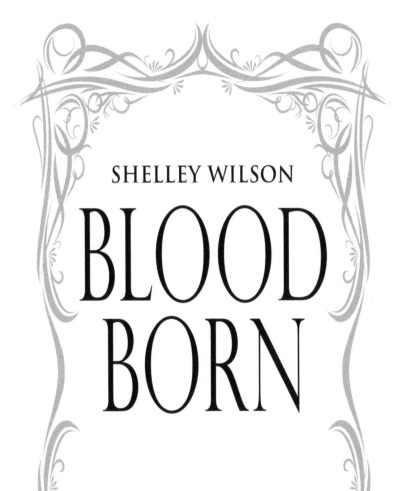

SHELLEY WILSON

BLOOD
BORN

bhc
press™

Livonia, Michigan

BLOOD BORN

Copyright © 2023 Shelley Wilson

This book is a work of fiction. The characters, incidents, and dialogue are drawn from the author's imagination and are not to be construed as real. Any resemblance to actual events or persons, living or dead, is entirely coincidental.

Published by BHC Press

Library of Congress Control Number:
2022941266

ISBN: 978-1-64397-340-1 (Hardcover)
ISBN: 978-1-64397-341-8 (Softcover)
ISBN: 978-1-64397-342-5 (Ebook)

For information, write:
BHC Press
885 Penniman #5505
Plymouth, MI 48170

Visit the publisher:
www.bhcpress.com

For my nephew, William.
Your thirst for reading is a delight
and an honour to be a part of.

BLOOD BORN

1

The big man's fist tightened around a length of her hair, pulling with every twist, while his breath closed in on her skin.

'No!' She heard the hitch in her voice as if someone else were speaking. It sounded distant, almost wretched. If it weren't for the pain shooting through her scalp, she might have laughed. Desperation was one of those emotions Emma had spent the last seventeen years running from. She'd swallowed any desire for warmth and compassion and kept tight control over any feelings of sentimentality. She knew people saw her as cold and reserved, but somewhere deep inside she knew it was vital for her survival to stay detached from those around her.

'But you smell so good,' the man's voice murmured into her ear from his secluded position behind her. 'Lonely girls taste the sweetest of all. They wallow in their isolation and let it envelop their souls. When I feed on them, it's like I'm high.'

'You don't have to do this!' Again with the whiny desperation. Was it so important that she stayed alive? Would anyone honestly care if she died tonight? Her racing thoughts settled on Flora, her grandmother by birth and her guardian by circumstance. Maybe Flora would welcome the news that she was free of her shackles, free of that obligation she had breathed into her daughter's ear in the maternity delivery room.

'Please!'

The man's laugh was empty of humour and raspy, like he smoked a hundred joints a day. As he licked the skin below her earlobe, his breath wafted over her, carrying a stench of rotting meat and something Emma couldn't place. She shuddered and tried to pull free of his ironclad grip as he dragged her head to the side. His other arm crossed her waist, pinning her arms to her sides with so much force it took her breath away.

'She told me you'd taste as sweet as a thunderstorm on a summer's day.' He trailed his tongue down her exposed neck.

'She? She who?'

Emma's unanswered question hung in the night air as the attacker bit down on her flesh. Red-hot pain ripped through her body with alarming speed, like railroad spikes being driven into her skin. Boiling heat rushed through her veins, sending every muscle in her body into spasm as Emma's heart fought against the vampire's venom. She couldn't break free or scream. She merely froze in his embrace as he sucked and tore at her throat.

As her pulse slowed and her body sagged against the powerful man who held her so tight, the soft suckling lulled her into a strange, hallucinogenic dream.

Floating. Falling. Dying.

The feel of his hard frame against her back vanished, and she slumped forward, landing heavily on her knees before pitching onto her face. The cold touch of the floor welcomed her as she slammed into it.

Struggling against the darkness that pushed at the outlying edges of her mind, Emma forced her eyes open and saw her attacker for the first time, standing a short distance away. His chiselled features contorted as his brow wrinkled and his sharp teeth disappeared into a now-slack mouth. A crimson stain from her blood coated his pale face and shirt.

Emma struggled to stay focused on the hole in his chest. A hooded figure stepped into view, smaller in frame than the man who had attacked her. The stranger held a bloody heart in their hand, its essence dripping onto the stone not far from where Emma lay with her face in the dirt. Then the vampire vanished in an explosion of crimson fireworks.

The stranger faded in and out of Emma's vision with every blink of her eyes. She couldn't make out their features or tell if they were male or female. Everything was blurring into a dark fog that she strained to resist. The image of the heart ripped from the man's chest became all-consuming. What power would it take to do such a thing? Was she next?

The hooded figure dropped by her side and rolled Emma over until she lay on her back.

Emma's eyes glazed over before refocusing on the blanket of stars above, as if seeing them for the first time. An entire blank canvas stretched out endlessly, and an unexpected calm washed over her. She was dying, and it was oddly peaceful despite the brutality of death.

The stranger sliced a thin blade across their wrist, drawing blood, and pressed it to Emma's parted lips. The blood loss she had endured made her weak, too weak to fight back, too weak to save herself from the horrors that were unfolding, and her feeble attempts at pushing the pale arm away were useless.

The coppery tang of blood filled her mouth, making her gag, but as she turned her head to the side to spit out the hot fluid, a strong hand clamped down over her nose and mouth, forcing her to swallow.

She tried to comprehend what was happening. Her logical mind was aware of her attacker's demise and the strange hooded figure, but the world was slowing down. Everything grew cold and dark; grey shadows danced in her peripheral vision.

Emma blinked, slowly, as she felt her life ebbing away.

• • •

The sound of voices whispering in the background was oddly soothing. Emma's mind raced as she forced her eyes open, squinting at the harshness of the fluorescent lights overhead. The room was small and stark; white walls and stainless steel units packed the space and a pale green curtain swished back and forth as a stream of people walked in and out. A strong smell of antiseptic burned her nostrils as a nurse came into view. The nurse felt for a pulse and shined lights into Emma's eyes until the brightness made her teeth ache.

The hushed conversations around her drifted in and out as she fought to remain conscious.

'Her neck was torn apart.'

'Blood everywhere!'

A loud thumping noise reverberated through the air as another nurse leaned in to check Emma's temperature. The nurse gave her a strained smile, and Emma realised with a jolt that she was hearing the sound of the nurse's heart beating in her chest. The rhythmic thud, thud, thud of blood being pumped around the woman's body crowded Emma's mind.

'It's okay, sweetie. You're in the hospital. We're going to take good care of you.'

Emma tried to move and winced, lifting her fingers gingerly to her neck where a wad of bandages covered her throat. It all rushed back to her in a violent wave of memories. Someone, or something, had attacked, bitten, and fed on her.

Her body spasmed as she attempted to lift herself off the bed. It took three nurses to pin her back down. Their soothing yet concerned voices grated on every nerve in Emma's body.

She tried to speak but only mustered a croak.

'Hush now. Don't talk. Your throat will be sore for a while as you heal. Just try to relax and let us do our job.'

The pillow was soft against her head as she slumped back onto the hospital bed, but there was no way she would ever be able to relax even if she wanted to.

Who had attacked her? Who had saved her? Why could she hear the beating of everyone's hearts like a symphony of drums? What was happening to her?

'She was dead at the scene.'

'How did she survive?'

She'd seen enough supernatural movies to piece it all together, but her brain rejected the outcome. It wasn't possible. If she was to believe the murmurs of the staff around her bed, then she had died tonight. Her attacker had bitten her, feeding on her blood until her heart slowed and she was on the verge of death, and then the mysterious stranger had forced her to drink their blood right before she took her last breath. To a lover of dark Gothic literature, it was obvious what had happened, but even as the words formed in her mind, Emma refused to accept them. She was a vampire.

A sharp scratch pulled at her attention, and she recoiled as the nurse punctured her skin, driving a needle into her vein. Panic swirled through her chest. What time was it? How long had she been there? Her heart must have stopped at least a few hours ago, which meant her blood would have begun to pool in her veins and arteries. Had she started to turn blue? She lifted her hand, but the skin was still a pale pink. She could still wiggle her fingers, so rigor mortis had not set in yet.

Whoever had fed her the blood was potentially a vampire, too, and if that were the case, she would have someone else's blood mingling with any she had left. Would that show up on a blood test? Would it raise red flags if her blood showed signs of death?

She yanked her arm away from the needle, knocking the nurse back a few paces.

No! Her vocal cords may have abandoned her, but from the wide-eyed stare the nurse gave her, she knew her disapproval registered.

'We'll do this later, sweetie. Don't you get yourself worked up about it. You've been through quite the ordeal.'

Did they know? Were they aware of the horror she had experienced?

Her eyes explored the room for a familiar face but only saw nurses and doctors with pursed lips and wrinkled brows. She felt like an exhibit in a zoo. As she wildly searched the sea of faces, she saw a boy standing beyond the door, his pale skin and red-rimmed eyes illuminated under the corridor light.

Emma grunted and motioned in his direction.

'Yes, he's the one who found you. Poor kid is still a bit shaken. He saved your life by getting you here so fast. He thought you were dead until you flinched and gave him one hell of a fright.'

Isolating herself throughout secondary school and college had felt like a necessary evil. Years spent blending into the background to watch and listen had earned Emma a catalogue of understanding about her fellow classmates. She knew who worked hard and who cheated. She had identified the popular kids and the loners, but occasionally, one of the nameless faces surprised her.

Paul Parker had been nice enough to her over the years despite his popularity and her weirdness. He never gave her the impression that he saw the darkness Emma carried in her heart. She kept her distance from everyone, choosing to internalise her feelings, cut herself off from the world, and battle the black fog that hovered around her on her own, but at that exact moment, she would have welcomed a friend.

Without a voice and separated by an ever-rotating army of hospital staff, she had no way of signalling Paul. He disappeared into the background as two police officers escorted him away, no doubt questioning him about the night's events. Emma surveyed the empty space he had occupied as the small screened-off hospital space became a mecca for every medical employee brave enough to seek out the girl with no blood in her system and no pulse to speak of.

She rested her head against the pillow to try to calm her whirling thoughts. Staring up at the ceiling didn't help. Nothing did. How was she ever supposed to make sense of what was happening to her?

Emma heard the commotion as if she were floating above it. The patter of rubber-soled shoes following the click of her grandmother's sensible heels drifted along the corridor, growing ever closer. Flora swooped into the hospital reception area with her forceful tone and confident air, demanding to see her granddaughter. She burst through the curtain separating Emma from the other patients with various injuries and ailments in the accident and emergency department. Emma couldn't help but smile at the artist smock covered in fresh paint and the wild wisps of grey hair framing her grandmother's face. Even in the middle of the night it seemed Flora's muse never stopped.

'What happened?' Flora demanded, turning on the nearest nurse, who jumped back as if dodging a bullet. Emma was used to Flora's abruptness, and she was painfully aware of Flora's ability to use that hard edge to her advantage. It was evident that Flora was in full theatrical flow, and this hospital room was her stage.

'We're not sure,' the nurse said as she approached the bed and pressed her fingers against Emma's wrist. 'Mrs Parker's son came across her in the alley. He thought she was dead. Scared the poor boy out of his wits.'

'Tsk!' Flora pushed the nurse aside and scooped Emma's hand into her own. Emma caught the slightest shift in Flora's posture as she touched Emma's cold skin. 'When can I take her home?'

A pensive expression settled on Flora's face as she avoided direct eye contact with Emma, turning toward the nurse instead.

'You can't take her home. We're still waiting for the doctor to run some tests.'

'What tests?'

The nurse took a deep breath, obviously used to dealing with impatient family members.

'We can't locate Emma's pulse, for one.'

Flora ran her fingers along Emma's arm, muttering under her breath as she did so. She gave Emma a look that would have silenced the dead, which seemed entirely appropriate under the circumstances.

'There,' Flora cried, turning back to the nurse. 'A pulse, as clear as anything.'

The nurse's brow creased as she stepped forward, but Flora was quick to push herself in between them.

'The girl is awake and responsive. Surely if she didn't have a pulse, it would mean she was dead! Does she look dead to you? No? Then I'm taking her home.'

Without waiting for an answer, Flora ripped the blanket away and carefully pulled Emma's legs over the edge of the hospital bed. Emma wasn't sure she had the strength to stand unaided, but before she had a chance to communicate her anxiety, Flora tugged her from the bed and she crashed to the floor.

'You!' Flora caught a porter by the arm as he trundled past the curtained room, pushing an empty wheelchair. 'Can we borrow that?'

He took one look at Emma and backed the chair alongside the bed.

'Flora, I really must insist that you wait for the doctor.' The nurse was losing her patience. 'Emma needs medical attention; a tetanus vaccine at least.'

'Nonsense. She's a strong girl. She just needs her bed and her nanna looking after her.'

Emma had never heard Flora refer to herself as a nanna before and realised she was using language the nurse would feel a connection with. Who wouldn't want their nanna looking after them? It worked, and the nurse moved to the side to let them pass.

'The police are interviewing Paul and will want to talk to Emma too. She's suffered a terrible ordeal, and if they're going to have any chance of catching the animal that attacked her, she'll need to give a statement.'

Flora's eyes shifted to her granddaughter's for the briefest of moments in silent understanding.

'Yes, yes, I'll be sure Emma gives the police all the assistance they need.' Flora waved her hand dismissively at the nurse.

'Be sure to bring her straight back if there's any sign of trouble,' the nurse shouted across the open reception area as Flora propelled the wheelchair with great haste toward the glass doors.

The night was fading into dawn as a morning chorus filled the sky above them. Flora had left her battered old MINI in the ambulance bay outside the entrance, and Emma wished she had the strength to shake her head in disappointment.

'Hurry! Get in the car.' Flora's voice was higher than normal as she bundled Emma into the passenger seat.

They tore through the streets at breakneck speed. Emma grasped her stomach, determined not to vomit in Flora's prized automobile.

'What's the rush?' Emma said in a raspy voice. Her throat was still raw where the attacker had bitten her.

'We need to get you inside quickly!'

Flora's cottage came into view as the first rays of dawn broke free.

Emma screamed as the sun lit up the sky, startling herself with the terrifying sound full of horror and pain. The agony in her head built in its intensity. It squeezed at her temples and it felt like her head was caught in a vice. Tears streamed down her face, but when she raised her hands to wipe them away, her fingers came back sticky with blood. She recoiled at the sight. Her vision swirled as a deep roaring sound wrapped her in a petrifying embrace, and her limbs trembled.

'What's happening?' The high, scratchy pitch in her voice forced Flora to mount the pavement and steer the small car between the hedges that surrounded the cottage. She slammed on the brakes, inches from the front door.

Flora yanked the car door open. Emma stumbled onto the path with her grandmother's help, blood trickling from her eyes and ears. The pain in her head was so unbearable she longed for the sweet embrace of death once again.

With shaking hands, Flora pushed the key in the lock and flung open the door to the cottage. She unceremoniously shoved Emma inside.

'Stay indoors,' Flora snapped, backing away. 'I'll return soon with something to help you.'

Just like that, Flora disappeared. Alone in the dark entrance hall, Emma slumped to the floor and cradled her head in her hands. Why was this happening?

The threadbare carpet was a welcome resting place as Emma tried to calm her breathing. She remained on the floor for what felt like hours, the pain in her head subsiding over time until she could hear her thoughts once more. Bringing her hand up to her neck, she tore the bandage away and touched the jagged flesh, wincing at the tenderness of the wound.

The previous night's attack rushed at her afresh, and she wept. Thankfully, this time there were tears instead of blood. She wasn't sure how to process what she'd seen, let alone what had happened to her. The attack was brutal, but what the hooded stranger had done was beyond cruel. Her memories ended with the stars blinking out, and then she'd awoken in a bright room with paramedics and nursing staff fussing over her, shaking their heads. The smell of blood was everywhere. It permeated her clothes, her hair, and the very air she breathed.

Blood.

Emma sniffed the air like she'd seen animals do when locating their prey on the television shows on Animal Planet. A strong smell wafted down the hall from the kitchen. Picking herself up from the carpet, she used the wall for support. Her stomach churned as she dragged her shaky frame across the hall.

She had grown used to dealing with life alone, cut off from her peers and teachers, but she couldn't understand why Flora had just left and abandoned her. It was obvious she needed help!

The kitchen was shrouded in darkness, the heavily patterned curtains obscuring the long garden and the beginning of a sunny day beyond. Her eyes darted around the room in search of the source of the smell. They settled on the joint of beef defrosting on the worktop. The lump of meat sat in a pool of blood on one of Flora's serving plates, the bright crimson a stark contrast to the purity of the white dish.

She lifted the plate to her lips and tried not to focus on the sloshing red fluid or why the juices were consuming her thoughts. She had to drink the blood; she *needed* to drink the blood.

As she drained the pungent liquid, the headache that still danced at her temples began to ease. Her grip loosened on the wall, and she stood unsupported. A surge of strength coursed through her. It reminded her of when she had accidentally touched an electrical socket with wet hands as a child and received a jolting shock.

Lapping up the meat's bloody extract brought with it two distinct emotions: fear and disgust. Emma threw the plate across the kitchen, where it clattered against the cupboard door and fell to the floor with a smash. The raw joint of meat bounced a few times before coming to a stop underneath the kitchen table. She had relished the taste of it, guzzled every drop until the plate was clean, and felt a satisfaction in the pit of her stomach that no cheeseburger had ever given her.

She sensed Flora walking down the front path before she registered the key in the lock. The front door opened with enough force to knock out a tooth if anyone had been standing behind it. Sunlight flooded the hall and dust particles sparkled in the disturbed air.

'What did you do?' Flora asked, her eyes darting around the kitchen. Emma wiped at her mouth with the back of her hand. It was stained with a smear of burgundy.

Emma stayed in the cool, dark embrace of the kitchen, wanting no part of the harsh, bright light at the front of the house. She watched her grandmother edge inside. Flora didn't leave the pool of light. Instead, she merely returned her granddaughter's gaze.

'You might need to buy another joint of beef,' Emma said. She lifted her fingers to touch the wound left by the vampire and noticed the tenderness in her neck and the damage to her throat no longer troubled her. There was no pain when she spoke, but Emma struggled to comprehend how that was possible. 'I couldn't stop myself. I drank the blood straight from the plate.'

'Tsk, I'm not surprised.' Flora slammed the door behind her.

Emma tensed as she smelt it again. Blood. Flora's blood. Her grandmother walked into the kitchen, forcefully dropping a bag on the kitchen table as she entered the room.

'Stay back!' Emma growled, gripping the edge of the worktop.

Flora obliged and moved to sit at the table. Emma wondered if Flora had strategically positioned herself close to the exit.

'I always feared this would happen one day,' Flora said at last. 'It's who you are, and I was kidding myself if I thought you'd never find out.'

Her words made no sense to Emma, and yet she had a compelling feeling that she was about to uncover at least one answer to the many questions that regularly crowded her overwhelmed brain. The hollow feeling in her chest was smaller somehow, like the blood had started to knit her insides back together.

'Do you know what's going on?' Emma asked.

Why wasn't Flora freaking out? How could she be so unmoved when Emma was bleeding from her eyes and show no surprise about her draining the bloody plate?

'You're a vampire, my dear girl. One of the undead.'

Hearing the words out loud made it sound even more ludicrous. Visions of Dracula and Lestat whirled around Emma's mind. She enjoyed watching horror and supernatural shows. The myths and legends of such creatures fascinated her, but they were exactly that: myths and legends.

'That's ridiculous!' She let out a loud, exasperated sigh. Emma retrieved the beef joint from the floor and threw it on the worktop before collecting the broken crockery and placing it in the bin. The action felt familiar, not unnatural. 'Vampires aren't real. They're the twisted imaginings of scriptwriters and Hollywood directors. They're a romantic notion invented for an army of girls to survive the crushing narcissism they deal with in high school. They're—' Her eyes fell on the bloody lump of meat. 'Why is this happening to me?'

'I have my suspicions, but I need to check out a few sources before I can confirm anything. I promise I'll explain everything, but for now, I need you to stay inside. Unlike those far-fetched shows you watch, you won't burst into flames in the garden, but as you now know, you'll have one hell of a headache if you stay in the sun too long without feeding.'

Recalling the pain and the blood oozing from her eyes and ears, Emma didn't need any further motivation to stay indoors. The chair's wooden legs scraped across the linoleum as she yanked it out from under the table and slumped onto the soft seat.

'It's like a bad dream! I feel like an unwilling cast member in *Night of the Living Dead*.'

Flora's face softened as she stretched her wrinkled hands across the table and covered Emma's pale, cold hands in a rare moment of affection.

'You're a special girl, Emma. Different from the other girls around here. Your mother wanted to keep you safe from those who might harm you, and she left me clear instructions. I thought I'd done my part in following them to the letter, but now—' She shook her head, and her unruly grey curls bounced back and forth. 'Now it looks like I'm the one who needs help.'

'You're not making any sense.' Frustration crept into Emma's voice as she scrutinised the millions of emotions rearranging her grandmother's craggy face. 'You can't get all cryptic on me now, not when my entire life is falling apart.'

'You're right.' Flora bounced up from the table, upending the contents of the shopping bag onto the wooden top. A blood bag tumbled out across the table. 'Be a dear and put this in the fridge. I'll be back later with the answers you need.'

'Where did you get that?' Emma cried. She spotted the Allendale Hospital crest on the package. 'Did you steal blood?'

'It's what you need. Everything has changed now, and I want you to trust that everything I do is to help you.'

The chair fell backwards as Emma stood and backed away from the table. The longer she stared at the bag of blood the more her hands trembled and shook.

'What the hell is going on, Flora?'

'Vampires drink blood—fact! You need to start thinking long term, Emma. Don't think about the source; just concentrate on your survival. Look, I'm out of my depth here and need to speak to my… friends.'

'Your friends? How the hell is your meditation circle going to help with *this*?'

'I have other sources with more experience in these kinds of situations.'

Emma laughed. How was it possible for anyone to have experience in vampirism?

'Stay here. I'll be back as soon as I can.'

'Wait! What am I supposed to do?'

'Rest. You'll need your strength. Just trust me that you'll be okay.'

With that, Flora hurried up the short hallway and out the front door. Emma heard her small heels clicking on the front path and the hum of the MINI's engine as it raced off down the street. She could still hear the car when Flora turned onto Hatton Terrace, four streets away.

What the hell? Emma shook her head as if to dislodge something inside and then sat in silence in the dark kitchen, listening to the outside world waking up.

Mr Walton was pulling his wheelie bin out to the side of the road and humming a tune. Mrs McCullen was walking her dog and talking to Mrs Parker on her mobile. Emma heard her own name. She closed her eyes and fixed her attention on the voices until she could hear clearly what they were saying.

'Poor Paul was still shaking when he got home,' Mrs Parker said. 'It turns out the Hartfield girl wasn't dead after all. Paul said she reeked of death though.'

'I'm outside their cottage now,' Mrs McCullen said. 'All the curtains are drawn, and Flora's car is gone.'

'Maybe the girl did die, and the old battle-axe has gone to bury her.'

The two women cackled, and Emma slumped into the seat, resting her head on the table. How could she hear them? Why could she smell the rotten vegetable peelings in Mr Walton's bin and the wet dog smell from Mrs McCullen's poodle?

Avoiding the bright strips of sunlight streaming through the cracks in the curtains and dappling the floor, she made her way upstairs to the bathroom and flicked on the shower. Paul Parker was right about one thing: she reeked of death.

The warm water cascading over her head calmed her whirling brain, washing away the grime from the alley, the scent of her attacker, and the blood—hers and that of the mysterious hooded stranger.

'Paul said she reeked of death.'

'We can't locate Emma's pulse.'

It was like a nightmare. Flora knew more than she was letting on, and Emma needed her more than ever. She was a vampire. She had died last night. Part of her wanted to grieve and scream, but the other part of her couldn't shake the strange feeling of acceptance bubbling up from the pit of her stomach.

Bundled up in a warm towel, she perched on the toilet seat and examined her hands. She had always been petite and slim, but her fingers were more elegant than she recalled. Her nails, usually bitten down to the quick, were glossy with perfectly rounded tips. The skin on her arms was paler than normal but blemish-free, as were her legs. Part of her didn't want to look in the mirror above the sink. What if the scriptwriters were right and a vampire had no reflection? She trembled as she stood and let the towel fall, exposing her naked body to the fluorescent bathroom light. The steam from the hot shower had misted the mirror, but as Emma wiped it clear, her reflection stared back. Relief flooded her system, and she snorted at the absurdity of needing to see herself. But what stared back chilled her to the core.

The girl in the mirror was slight of frame and had bony shoulders, small breasts, and a nipped-in waist. Her long dark hair hung wet and limp but was fuller than before, thicker perhaps. Her eyes still shone deep brown, but now they were a richer, more vibrant shade of brown if that were possible. She stood taller and with more confidence. It took Emma a while to remember that it was *her* reflection she was staring at; however, this girl looked like an ice queen, a distant and cold relative who had kept to the shadows all her life because she felt different. Emma related to her.

The darkness she had always felt around her no longer loomed like a predator—it swirled through her veins and fed her senses. An inner strength she had never experienced settled in the hollow space within her chest, giving her a sensation of completeness.

Two tiny puncture wounds on her neck were the only remaining evidence of the vicious attack—her murder no less. She had died out there in the alley, under the blanket of stars, with a stranger's blood flooding through her system.

Heavy footsteps pounded up the front path, and Emma braced herself for the knock on the door. The sound boomed like a cannon and grated on her nerves, leaving her head bursting. All her senses were heightened, yet she had no idea how to control them. A simple tap on the front door sounded like an explosion. How was she supposed to cope with that?

'Emma? Are you there?'

Paul Parker's voice shocked her into movement, and she grabbed a robe to cover her naked body. They had grown up in the same town, attended the same schools and college, and he'd now seen her at her worst—dead—yet a tiny spark of the old Emma wanted him to see her as a normal girl still.

The rising sun was shifting, which meant she could open the front door without fear of a migraine and bleeding from her eyes and ears—something she was sure Paul Parker wouldn't relish after the shock of finding her in a bloody heap.

'Hello.' She clung to the door as she greeted him, digging her nails into the wood. He was in his running gear and beads of sweat glistened on his forehead while his heart beat loudly.

'I hope you don't mind me coming to see you.' He took a small step forward. 'I was out for a run, and when I saw I was near your house, I wanted to check that you were okay.'

Blood. Sweat. Beating heart.

'I'm fine now, thank you.' She had to dig deep to stop herself from dragging him through the front door and tearing into his flesh. The only problem was another rage was also building inside her. One that she didn't understand and had nothing to do with the fact that she was now a vampire. Paul had found her in the alley, and he was the one who had alerted the police and phoned an ambulance. He was her saviour, not her attacker, and yet the growing fury felt like hot sweat rising from her toes. She knew this pain and anger was not directed at Paul but at the man who'd hurt her. Focusing all her efforts, she took a deep breath in, and like drinking a cooling glass of water, she dampened the heat coursing through her veins until she was more in control and able to speak again.

It dawned on her then that Paul would have seen her attacker's body in the alley.

'What happened to the man who attacked me?' It hadn't occurred to her to ask this simple question before. Flora hadn't given her any time to explain what had happened before leaving her to cope alone.

Paul's forehead crumpled, and he took yet another step forward. Emma braced herself against the wood and blocked the entrance with her body.

'The police aren't looking for a person. They said it was probably a wild dog.'

She stared at him for a long moment as she processed what he was saying. How many feral dogs were there in Allendale?

'No, that's not right.' She released her grip on the door and it swung open, accidentally initiating an invitation to the boy on her front step.

Paul strode inside and walked down the hall before Emma could stop him. She was vaguely aware that he had visited her home once before, with his mother, for a herbal remedy that Flora had made to help with some illness. She heard the beat of his heart slow as he entered the kitchen and knew he felt welcomed and relaxed. Emma skirted past him and scooped up the blood bag, dropping it into her pocket before motioning for him to take a seat. Paul sank into a kitchen chair and smiled up at her.

'What's not right?' he asked.

'It wasn't a dog that attacked me. It was a man. He spoke to me. I saw him.'

Paul shook his head. 'I can only tell you what I saw and what the police said at the scene. They took samples of blood from the ground, but they were pretty convinced that an animal bit you. I didn't see any sign of a man, only you.'

She lowered herself into the chair opposite Paul and let his words wash over her. Had she imagined the man, the attack, and the hole in his chest where his heart had once sat? Had she dreamt up the mysterious hooded person who had fed her their blood?

'They're covering it up,' she muttered under her breath. 'They don't know how to explain what happened.'

'Finding you in that alley was pretty horrific. There was so much blood, and you were so pale.' Paul's voice drifted into silence, and she glanced up at him when she caught the hitch in his pulse. Tears pooled in his eyes, but he wiped them away with the sleeve of his running shirt. 'Sorry, I've never seen a dead body before.'

Emma laughed, but there was no joy in it. 'Not dead, Paul. I'm sitting right in front of you.'

It was his turn to laugh, but he put more feeling into it. 'You looked pretty damn dead last night.'

She had known Paul Parker since they were children and had always thought he was good-looking, but as she watched him glance around her kitchen, her thoughts were focused on the pumping of blood through his body. The vein in his neck pulsed under the dim kitchen light. Emma's mind conjured up the image of her cradling his head in her hands and sinking her teeth into his throat.

'Emma? You okay?'

'What?' She regained her composure and tried to avoid focusing on his neck. 'Yes, a bit dazed, I guess. The hospital said I lost a lot of blood, so I'm still spaced-out.'

'I get it. You've been through a rough time, but I want you to know that you can talk to me any time you want.'

Flora interrupted his kind words, bursting through the back door with a loaded rucksack that Emma somehow knew contained more blood bags.

'What's going on?' Her voice was shrill, almost panicked, as she glanced between her granddaughter and Paul.

'Hey, Flora. I wanted to check in on Emma and see how she was.' Paul rose from his seat and started to help Flora with her bag until she shooed him away.

'Right, of course. How thoughtful of you.' She dumped the rucksack on the floor and slid it under the table with her foot. 'But I really think Emma needs her rest. It's been an eventful few hours.'

Her eyes sparkled with something akin to pride as her gaze drifted between Emma and Paul, but it was so fleeting Emma assumed she was imagining it.

'You're right,' he said, moving back down the hallway toward the front door. 'I'll catch up with you again soon, Emma.'

She lifted her hand in a half-hearted wave as Flora hustled him outside and slammed the door shut.

'You are astounding,' Flora said as she bustled back into the kitchen. 'I've never heard of anything like it from a new vampire.'

'Heard what?'

'You were chatting.'

She said it like it was the strangest thing two human beings might do.

'Yes, it's a modern concept.' Emma realised Flora rarely held civil conversations and had therefore forgotten the art. 'When two people have known each other for years, they chat.'

'New vampires don't chat! New vampires are unpredictable, cold, and violent. They drain the blood from unsuspecting humans, leaving a trail of corpses in their wake, whether they're acquainted or not. Humans are nothing more than a meal to a new vampire.'

Until that moment, Emma hadn't thought it possible to feel any colder, but a chill travelled through her that knocked any remaining breath from her body.

'I would never—' Emma couldn't believe that Flora, her own flesh and blood, would ever think she could harm anyone.

'I know you wouldn't want to hurt that boy, but when you're a newly turned vampire, you lose all sense of what's right. You're overcome by darkness.'

There—a piece of the puzzle. Darkness was an old friend of hers. She had already embraced that part of herself, and perhaps it had helped her transition into a new kind of monster. A monster that should prey on the innocent but instead passed the time with polite conversation. Had she been lulling Paul into a false sense of security only to drink from his carotid artery later? Her stomach churned at the thought.

'If you take anything from this experience, let it be your strength and resilience,' Flora said with a fiery edge to her words. 'You are truly special.'

'I'm a bloody vampire! That's not special. It's demonic.' She jumped from the chair, knocking it back into the cupboards behind her with a deafening thump. 'I died last night, and nobody knows it— not Paul, not the police, nor the hospital staff. They're all going about their business, totally oblivious to the fact that—'

Dead. It was so final. She had lost both her parents—her father dying before she was born, and her mother dying as she brought Emma into this world—and now she had lost herself. How was it possible that she was still walking and talking? Tears tumbled down her cheeks as the reality hit home. Nothing would ever be the same again.

'You've always been a special girl, Emma. But this new development means you're also valuable to many other people—bad people— and that's why I need to tell you everything.'

The sincerity in her grandmother's voice surprised her. Flora had always been so detached around Emma, letting her do her own thing and make her own choices, as if it were a hardship to be saddled with the responsibility of caring for her. Flora had a full and active life with many friends and weekly clubs, and she had made it clear early on that Emma wasn't going to get in the way of her enjoying her life. Hearing Flora speak so gently and honestly made it all the harder to accept. Now, she seemed like a stranger.

'Tell me what?' Emma asked.

'It's time you discovered who Emma Hartfield really is.'

2

'I'll only be gone for a couple of days,' Flora had told her as she packed the fridge with blood bags.

After resisting the urge to murder Paul Parker, Emma had accepted that a few days without her grandmother shouldn't cause her too much distress.

She couldn't argue with her for leaving her alone this time as Flora's trip carried the hope of getting answers about who had attacked her and why. Flora kept her sources anonymous, and Emma tried not to think too much about how her grandmother knew anything about a world with vampires in it. Flora's assurances that she would explain everything and get the help and information they needed was enough—for the moment.

Now, as she listened to the hushed conversations in the coffee shop, Emma began to rethink the confidence she had in her ability of restraint.

She was testing herself to see how strong her control was over the vampire urges, and it was getting harder with every passing second.

Sitting in a crowded coffee shop surrounded by her neighbours wasn't something Emma had ever thought she would find uncomfortable, until now. The smell of their blood mixed with the scents of coffee beans, perfume, sweat, and cinnamon. It overwhelmed her.

One coffee. That was her limit.

'She looks very pale.'

'The police officer at the scene said it was the worst attack they had seen in years.'

A tiny crack trailed up the side of the mug as her grip tightened, and a trickle of muddy liquid leaked onto the tabletop. Small-town gossip was what these people did best, but Emma hated being the subject of their mindless chatter. She prided herself on being the nobody, the ghost girl who slipped under the radar and was quickly forgotten.

Every eye in the room turned toward her as she rose to leave. She kept her head down, mumbled a thank you to the barista, and hurried through the door and out to the street.

The air was crisp, and she sucked in a great lungful of it to calm herself. Even though she technically didn't breathe anymore, this simple act still comforted her.

Despite the murmurs and the strange looks from everyone, she was proud of herself. She had controlled the darkness within and sat amongst the population—something Flora had told her was impossible for a new vampire. She had proven she wasn't a danger to her neighbours, and now she hoped her grandmother would prove that Emma wasn't a danger to herself.

How the old lady knew so much and had kept these things to herself for seventeen years baffled Emma, but in a warped way, she was grateful to her attacker for forcing the truth into the world.

Home was a short stroll away, and walking was such a regular, human act that she had never considered it dangerous before. Surviving an hour in the coffee shop had been easy; now she needed to survive the walk home. Despite being a fierce killing machine— Flora's words—she couldn't shake the memory of her attack. Now she was more aware of who walked behind her, how they breathed, where they placed their feet on the pavement, and a hundred other intricacies that no human ever considered.

Every human action also had consequences. Even though she had told Flora she would never have hurt Paul or anyone else, Emma had to appreciate that she didn't know what she was capable of. The possibility of causing someone pain was now a reality.

Raised voices interrupted her thoughts, and she adjusted her sensitive hearing to focus on heated words being exchanged near the entrance to the park. The tall shrubs gave way to an open space close to the football pitches where three larger boys were pushing and shoving a much smaller lad.

A wave of anger like red mist flooded her system, and before she thought about approaching them, she was standing in front of the weaker youngster, offering a protective screen.

'What's going on?'

'None of your business, zombie girl.' The boys snickered and nudged one another.

Being such a small community, news of her attack and subsequent rising from the dead had swarmed through the neighbourhood. The schoolkids were running with the story before her scar had even healed, calling her a zombie that would bring about the end of days in Allendale. If only they knew how close to the truth they were.

Emma ignored their sneers. 'I'll ask you one more time. What's going on?'

The biggest of the three ambled forward. He had dirty brown hair matted across his acne-riddled forehead. His coat flapped around his protruding belly, and the stench of body odour made Emma gag.

Bypassing her, the boy sidestepped to eyeball the child she was protecting. 'There's nowhere for you to run, you little shit.'

The sound of the smaller boy's pounding heart boomed in her ears as Emma bunched her hands into fists.

'You touch one hair on this kid's head, and you'll have me to deal with.' Her gums itched as she stared at the three bullies in front of her.

They laughed, and the sound grated on her last nerve.

'Who died and made you the boss?' More snickering and congratulating each other on their timely comeback.

With extraordinary speed, Emma dragged the spotty youth to the ground and loomed over him with a hiss, straddling his malodorous body with his coat bunched up in her fists. His eyes widened in shock as she leaned in close. The sound of his heart and pulse speeding up filled her with satisfaction.

'I said, leave him alone!' The other boys backed away as she turned her head. The terror on their faces gave Emma the jolt she needed to assess her actions. To a neutral observer, she must have looked like a predator hunched over a fresh kill.

She let go of the boy and stumbled backwards, her head spinning at what she could have done. Running her tongue along her gums, she felt a sharp fang and clamped a hand over her mouth. The three boys ran off, away from the park entrance, and away from Emma. She tasted their fear on the wind.

Realising that she might have also scared their young victim, she spun toward him but found the space empty. He had clearly escaped at the first opportunity, and she hoped he had not witnessed her spiral from protector to hunter.

She craved the sanctuary of her home, and was once again reminded of Flora abandoning her when she needed help. It was becoming more important for Emma to make sense of all this and to deal with the changes. Allendale was a small town, and if she started to terrorise the community, then it would cause more trouble than either of them could handle.

Their house came into view, and Emma was relieved to see Flora's car in the driveway. She began to mentally prepare herself for whatever news her grandmother was about to share. Legacies, vampire lore, and bloodlust were conversation starters she'd never thought she would need to use in this lifetime, but she was prepared to stay open-minded.

The muted aroma of sandalwood, Flora's favourite incense, hit her as she opened the front door. The scent brought a million childhood memories tumbling to the forefront of her mind every time she smelt it.

The life of an orphan girl should have turned out differently, but Flora had become mother, father, and mentor. Eccentricities and aloofness aside, the quirky old lady with her long, ruffled skirts, wild grey curls, and crystal bracelets snaking up her arms was all Emma had.

'Flora, I'm home.'

Silence greeted her, which was not unusual as Flora's hearing was questionable these days. The broken crockery on the floor and the upturned wooden kitchen chair were out of the ordinary though. The delicate pattern of Flora's favourite china teacup shimmered on the ground, catching Emma's eye.

'Flora! Where are you?'

Emma scooped up the shattered remains and dumped them in the rubbish bin as she left the kitchen, an unsettling feeling of panic igniting every nerve in her body. She entered the living room, a space that usually exuded tranquillity and an overabundance of angel figurines.

'What the hell?'

The plush velvet cushions from the sofa were scattered across the floor and partially buried beneath the old sideboard that Flora had brought back from France. The cupboard now lay on its side. Its glass facade was broken, and the contents had spilled from the shattered frames. Angels, crystals, and fairies crunched beneath her shoes as she walked toward the staircase in the far corner of the room that led to Flora's bedroom.

Blood.

She smelt it before she saw the dark streaks on the handrail.

'Flora!' Panic consumed her as she raced up the stairs two at a time.

The carnage continued upstairs, with every drawer and cupboard ransacked. Emma's chest tightened as she turned in a full circle, taking in the destruction of their home. Flora's overnight bag lay discarded on the bed, a sign that she had made it this far before this devastation unfolded.

Emma sniffed the blanket at the foot of the bed and picked up Flora's strong aroma—a mix of spices and sunflowers. Using her newfound smelling superpower, she began to track the scent. Down the stairs, through the living room, into the kitchen, and out the back door. Emma ran to the end of the garden where the gate stood ajar, leading to the small service road.

'Damn it.'

The warm, spicy scent vanished as it blended with petrol and rubber. Emma glanced down the empty street. A rising sense of fear bubbled in her stomach. Who would want to kidnap an old lady?

The sunlight prickled her skin, and although she knew she wouldn't burst into flames, she still needed to drink blood to prevent the crippling migraine and the bleeding the sun's rays could inflict. Five days had passed since she had become a vampire, but she had already learned her lesson. Drinking her full quota for the day was critical.

The safety of the house beckoned, and she rushed inside, slamming and bolting the door behind her. Her ground-floor bedroom was decorated in pale green. The colour had calmed her as a child and had continued to relax her as a young adult. She had added posters, shelves, and potted plants over the years, enhancing the tranquillity of the room. Today it felt far from peaceful.

Even her bedroom hadn't escaped the intruder's reach. Her clothes had been dragged from the cupboards and strewn across the floor. The flowering cactus Flora had bought for Emma's last birthday was balanced precariously on its side. Soil had spilled across the desk and onto the carpet.

She sat on the end of her bed and surveyed the space. The destruction had touched every part of her room. Pots were upturned, furniture was broken, and most of her things were out of place. The wooden photo frame on her nightstand caught her eye. Someone had laid it flat on the surface, hiding the photo, but the glass was still intact. She picked it up, studying one of the few photographs she had of her and Flora together. Emma had taken the selfie one summer in the garden, capturing Flora as she had tended to her herbs. They had enjoyed the sunshine together that day. Both were tanned from the glorious weather they had been experiencing, and both were smiling.

She loved this photo. Sniffing the frame, she thought she recognised the odd scent. It seemed familiar. Did someone she know cause this destruction? Could it be possible that someone from Allendale was responsible for this? Would they harm an old lady?

Her shoes ground the spilled soil into the threadbare carpet as she marched out of the room and back into the kitchen. She felt useless sitting at home after her unsuccessful search in the daylight. She hadn't fed enough today, and the itch beneath her gums had begun to irritate her. Perhaps that was why she had lost it with the boys in the park. Being in the sunlight without enough blood running through her system could be catastrophic.

She jumped to attention when she sensed someone walking down the front path. His scent and the steady beat of his heart were becoming as natural to her as her own reflection.

'What do you want, Paul?' she growled, wrenching the door open before he knocked.

He leapt back with a yelp, and Emma felt a tremor of guilt for startling him.

'I'm sorry, Emma. I just wanted to check in on you.'

'It's not a good time, Paul. Flora is missing. You haven't seen her, have you?'

'Not since yesterday.' His heart beat a steady rhythm, and she knew he wasn't lying. 'Has she gone to one of her retreats and forgotten to tell you?'

'Possibly.' Emma didn't want to admit her fears.

'Do you want me to help you find her?'

She knew he was angling for an invitation inside, but she couldn't let him see the carnage and destruction of their home. Every fibre of her being wanted to reach out to him and ask for help, but she remained steadfast in the doorway.

'Thanks, but you're probably right about her being on one of her jaunts.'

Paul scanned the road beyond, where a group of girls were walking and chatting.

His heartbeat lifted ever so slightly as the group of girls drew closer, and she was acutely aware of a shift in his testosterone levels. He'd always been confident, but right now, he oozed arrogance. Emma realised with startling clarity that his status in town must have been elevated after finding her body in the alley and saving her with his quick actions.

The attack had ripped her world apart. She had let her ice-queen guard down and almost let Paul Parker inside her impenetrable emotional walls. She studied the handsome boy standing on her front step, with his back straight and his chin held high. He was lapping up the glory at her expense.

She was tempted to accept his help to find Flora, but she would be forcing him into a world of vampires, blood, kidnappings, and trashed homes. Despite her newly simmering loathing for Paul Parker, she didn't relish the idea of him being a part of her messed-up life.

'Shout if you need anything. I'm always here for you, Emma.'

He strolled down the path to catch up with the girls, who were waiting beyond the hedge for their hero of the hour.

The urge to drag him into the hedge and rip his throat out surprised Emma and spurred her into movement. She slammed the door.

Paul was harmless. He was a cute guy who liked to be the centre of attention. It seemed like he'd dated about 90 per cent of the girls in their grade, yet somehow, he was now single. Maybe he was losing his charm as he got older. Emma couldn't blame him for using her attack to boost his profile. She should applaud him for the way he had turned such a horrific event into a dating strategy.

At least he was still alive.

• • •

Emma dug through the papers in Flora's faded bureau. She was surprised to discover just how many secrets her grandmother had been keeping from her. There were records about her birth that a surgeon had sent directly to Flora, bypassing the paediatrician at their local surgery. The notes talked about Emma's safety for the future and included a cryptic message about never telling her the whole truth.

None of it made any sense. Flora had always said Emma's mother had lost too much blood when bringing her into the world and had faded away before the nurses were able to resuscitate her. The surgeon's scribbles hinted at something much darker. He wrote about her birth like it was some kind of miracle—a once-in-a-lifetime experience for him—and how her mother's sacrifice should never be forgotten.

She came across a journal that looked like it had been written by Flora and contained some illustrations and a list of family names and crests.

Hartfield
Astley
Deveroux
Byron

She had thought that once Flora returned, she would get some answers as to why this had happened to her. Now the bubbling questions were multiplying by the second, and she was having to deal with it alone.

Flora was gone. Perhaps the mysterious hooded figure, who had forced their blood into Emma's mouth, had taken her grandmother. What if they were in the process of turning Flora too?

She went to the kitchen, grabbed a blood bag, and ripped off the tab, pouring the contents into a black mug to disguise what it was. Her head fought against the unnatural sensation of drinking blood. She had to force her brain to compartmentalise everything to be able to swallow and keep the liquid down. Feeding was how she would build her strength and, in turn, how she would muster all the might she would need to find and save Flora. She didn't have to like it though.

A sharp knock at the door startled her, and she mentally kicked herself for internalising instead of staying aware of her external environment. Another attack could come at any moment, and she was too busy tempering her queasy nature to notice.

The person standing beyond the closed door was a stranger. She didn't recognise their scent, and she couldn't register their heart rhythm, unlike Paul Parker, whose heartbeat she could pick out from three streets away. Her hand hovered over the handle for a moment as she collected herself, preparing to either fight or flee.

Legs and hair were the first things that registered when she swung the door open. The woman on the doorstep was tall, at least six feet. She wore knee-high boots that hugged her calves and tight black trousers that made her legs look like stilts. Her face was turned away from the door, but her Afro curls seemed to move independently as she spun around, as though they were alive. Emma had to resist the urge to reach out and touch them. The mysterious woman was wrapped in a teal jacket with a fake fur collar. She clutched a clipboard to her side, and her nails were perfectly manicured.

'Hello,' the woman said brightly. 'Do you have a spare moment to complete a questionnaire for me? It's for charity.'

Emma blinked. Had ordinary just come crashing down on her dangerously abnormal life?

'I don't really have time.' Emma started pushing the door closed on the woman's smiling face.

'Oh, I'm sure you've got a couple of minutes.' The woman halted the door's closure with her free hand. 'After all, charity starts at home, doesn't it, Emma?'

The stranger was inside before Emma could stop her. She strode toward the kitchen like an old friend who popped over all the time.

'Need a hand tidying up? Looks like you've had quite the encounter.' Emma remained rooted to the spot by the front door.

Some people talk about leaving their body and floating above it while in the operating theatre, and Emma imagined that experience would be similar to this one. The beautiful stranger was picking up furniture and clearing away broken crockery, while Emma felt incapable of movement.

'Leave it!' Emma recovered from her trancelike state and slammed the front door. 'Who the hell are you, and what do you want?'

'I'm Cara.' The woman extended her hand for Emma to shake. It was an interesting test. Emma knew as soon as she touched her, this stranger would know Emma was different. Her skin was ice cold—a clear sign that she was a vampire. Was that Cara's plan? Was she a hunter of some kind? Emma stared at Cara's hand but refused to shake it. Instead, she scooped up one of the kitchen chairs and sat at the table. Cara lowered her hand and gave a small smile before following Emma's lead and sitting opposite her.

'How do you know who I am?'

Cara placed her clipboard on the table and clasped her hands together on top of it.

Instead of answering her with words, Cara smiled, and two fangs slipped into place. Emma jumped back from the table, causing her chair to clatter to the floor.

'You're a vampire!'

'Yes, I'm a vampire. I've been a vampire for a very long time, and I think I can help you with your current situation.'

'What do you know about my current situation?' Was this the mysterious hooded stranger who had turned her? No, she was way too tall; that person had been roughly the same height as Emma. Maybe she was the person who had instigated the attack and told the vampire that Emma would taste as sweet as a thunderstorm on a summer's day.

'Emma, I need you to calm down. Your thoughts are jumbled, and it's impairing your judgement. I'm not the enemy.'

'You can read my thoughts?'

'I can catch snippets or the odd word. Over the years, I've honed my skills to include reading people and interpreting their body language. You'd be amazed how much you can learn from just observing.'

Realising she had thrust herself flat against the opposite wall, Emma tried to relax her frame and inched back toward the table.

'We know about every vampire in the country. It's our job to stay connected with the underworld and keep it, and the human world, safe,' Cara continued.

'I don't understand why this is happening to me.' Emma paced the kitchen as she spoke. 'I was attacked, and now I find out there are more people like me.'

'Yes, I'm a vampire, but I'm not *exactly* like you.'

'What the hell does that mean?'

'I'm a half-blood—bitten and turned when I was twenty-seven—but you're different...special.'

Alarm bells went off in Emma's head, and the room started spinning as she slumped into a chair. Flora had said the same thing only a few days before, but she had also said that evil people thought she was valuable. Was Cara one of these bad people? Emma couldn't understand how being attacked and turned into a vampire made her special. She wasn't sure she wanted to find out, especially if it had already endangered Flora.

'Why do people keep saying that? It makes no sense. There's nothing special about me. You've obviously got the wrong person. Five days ago, I was just a girl, keeping myself to myself and staying out of trouble, and then some maniac attacked me in the street.'

'We haven't gotten it wrong, Emma. You're the one I'm here for. I'm part of a group called the Haven, and we're here to ensure the safety of all vampirekind.'

Emma prompted her to keep talking.

'I'm sure you have many questions, and all will be answered in time. For now, I need you to come with me so we can keep you safe.'

'I can't. Someone has taken my grandmother, and I need to find her.'

'If your grandmother has been taken, then you are compromised. It's dangerous for you to be on your own right now.'

Leave Allendale? After her altercation in the park earlier, there was a strong possibility that an angry mob carrying pitchforks would drive her out of town. Leaving with a woman she had only just met—a vampire—when her grandmother was missing wasn't an option, and she still had a million unanswered questions.

'I can't go with you. I need to find Flora.'

'We can find her together. The Haven has the resources you need to locate your grandmother, and I have the perfect team to get her back.'

Emma's body tensed as the vampire touched her arm.

'I know you find it hard to trust, Emma, but I need you to believe that I am here to help. The Haven can offer you sanctuary, and my friends can become your friends.'

Cara's head spun to the door right before the loud rap on the wood echoed through the house.

'Get rid of them,' Cara hissed. Her eyes flashed red for the briefest of moments.

Part of Emma hoped it would be Flora having forgotten her key, but the nearer she got to the door, the stronger his scent became.

'What do you want now, Paul?' Emma yelled through the wood. 'I told you now wasn't a good time.'

'How did you know it was me?' He laughed, but there was no humour in it.

'Go away, Paul.'

'*Please*, Emma. I need you to open the door.'

His heart was racing, and she longed for Cara's skill of partially reading someone's thoughts.

Her instinct overtook common sense, and she yanked open the door to find Paul standing on the doorstep with sweat soaking the front of his T-shirt and under his armpits. He squinted at her as he wrinkled his brow. He had no smile for her this time, only a twitch of his lips. She knew he hadn't been on another run as he was still wearing his jeans. He obviously wasn't sweating because of exercise, yet he trembled as though he had just finished a rigorous workout.

'What do you want?' She was talking to Paul, but her senses were on full alert, taking in every centimetre of air around him. Paul's arms jerked at his sides, shaking uncontrollably. His hair was ruffled like it had been caught in a breeze even though there was none. 'What's the matter?'

'I don't know.' A single tear trailed down his cheek. 'I was told to come here and get you to come outside. That's all they said.'

'That's all who said?'

She felt it then, the sensation of being watched. The house was shielded by an evergreen hedge and wasn't visible from the front, so she knew it couldn't be one of the neighbours peeking from their curtains. She didn't see anyone out on the street. A shudder ran down her spine.

'Come inside.' She reached out to take hold of Paul's hand and tugged him forward, but he didn't move. It was like he was cemented to the front step.

'I'm so sorry, Emma.'

From behind him a dark shape broke free and lunged forward. Emma screamed and pivoted backwards using the front door as a springboard. Without thinking, she launched herself beyond Paul and into the path of a weasel-faced man with a sprinkling of hair on his chin and a long scar above his right eye. He looked to be about her age, but the wicked glint in his expression suggested he was older than his apparent age. A deep crimson rimmed his eyes, giving him a serial-killer vibe. No wonder Paul was in such a state. Her messed-up life had managed to find Paul Parker after all.

'What do you want?'

The boy's feral smile took her back to the alley. The memory of her attacker's voice in her ear and his fangs at her throat filled her mind. Was this another attempt to murder her? Had the mysterious stranger interrupted a kill order, and now they, whoever they were, had sent a second team?

The hooded person wasn't there to save her today; it was up to Emma. The boy sprang forward with his fists bunched, but she dodged the move and brought her knee up into his groin. He grunted, stumbling, but recovered swiftly and circled back around for another assault. Instinct overtook her limbs, and she punched him square in the face as he ran at her. As he rebounded, she grabbed his arm and swung him in a semicircle, slamming him against the wall of the house. Flora's garden rake rested against the hedge, and in one fluid movement, Emma broke the handle in two and drove one end into the boy's chest.

She had seen it a million times on the screen, that moment when a vampire disappears in a cloud of dust, but the reality was far worse. The boy screamed so loud she thought her eardrums would burst. He began convulsing, and blood oozed out of his nose, mouth, and eyes as he slumped to the ground. The horror transfixed her. The vampire's skin bubbled and fizzed until the inevitable end when his body exploded. She had expected particles of dust, but she ended up covered in a red mist of fine ichor.

The loud sob behind her tugged her attention from the horror of the vampire's demise. Paul Parker was no longer rooted to the spot and had ventured forward a step or two to take in the spectacle. How was she ever going to explain this?

'What—'

He didn't need to say anything else. Emma got it. No words could explain what he had just witnessed.

'Are you okay? Did he hurt you?'

Paul shook his head as Cara strolled out of the house. She eyed the vampire mist coating Emma's clothes with distaste but headed straight for Paul. Her long fingers gripped his chin, forcing him to look at her.

'You were never here,' she said in a low voice, her face two inches from Paul's. 'You saw Emma and Flora leave for a short holiday by the sea. You wished them well, and then you left. Do you understand?'

'I...understand. Yes.'

She released his face and turned him toward the gate. Without a second glance, he marched off down the street.

'What did you do to him?'

'A kind of hypnosis,' Cara said. 'It's for their own benefit. If humans got involved in our world, it would be too dangerous for them.'

She knew Cara was right, but watching Paul walk away still stung. He might have his flaws, like using her attack for his own gain, but he was a connection to the other Emma, the human Emma. It was difficult to break free of that.

'I'm not sure it's such a good idea for me to go with you. There's a darkness about me that causes anyone in my path to either leave or get hurt.' Emma pointed at the crimson stain on the grass for emphasis.

'That darkness you talk about is part of who you are. Before your attack it would have remained dormant deep inside of you, niggling away like an untreatable rash, but now it's free, isn't it? Now you're free, and it's time to claim those dark roots and turn them into a powerful weapon against evil.'

Emma stared into the deep brown eyes of this beautiful stranger, the red glow from earlier now a distant memory. A tiny flame ignited within her chest. If Cara was telling the truth, then the Haven might be the only place she would find answers and the help she needed. It was obvious that she wouldn't find Flora on her own; she couldn't even decipher Flora's notebooks. Perhaps now was the time to try something new.

'Okay. I'll come with you, but only if you can help me find Flora.'

'The Haven will help you, and hopefully, you'll also learn to accept that you have friends.'

Friends. Such an alien word. She had been cut off for so long that she found it hard to believe anyone would want to be her friend. Did she even know how to let someone in?

'Yeah, we'll see.'

Cara didn't seem to notice her inner turmoil at the thought of meeting new people and sharing her life with them.

'Let's get you cleaned up, shall we?' Cara turned to face Emma. 'You'll learn about vampire lore and how to deal with these situations in time.' She waved her hand in the direction of the red stain that had once been a vampire. 'And we'll teach you how to use your powers. When we get to the Haven, the council leaders will want to meet you.

They'll have questions for you, but don't worry, I'll be there to guide you. My team will try to keep the excitement to a minimum.'

Emma stared at her as if she were speaking Swahili.

'What makes me so special?'

'You really don't know, do you?'

Emma shook her head, more confused than ever.

'You'll find out soon enough.'

Cara's sudden desire to clean the front garden made it clear the conversation was over. Emma guessed the answers she sought would be found at the Haven. Until she discovered why someone had turned her and why her human grandmother had been kidnapped, she would be in the dark. Without all the facts, Emma was vulnerable, and that bothered her. Perhaps it was time to place some trust in other people and hope they offered the assistance she needed. She had to believe that she wasn't walking into more trouble than she could handle.

3

The stars shone so much brighter once they were away from the city. They drove down unlit back roads, winding through the countryside. Emma marvelled at how much sharper her senses were while she watched the blackness of the fields and lanes rush past the car window. For the first time, she almost appreciated her vampire gifts. So far, all she had felt was repulsion, anger, and a thirst that left her lightheaded if she didn't feed, but right now she was content.

'Are you going to tell me where we're going?' They had been driving for hours with barely a word exchanged for most of the journey. Emma was grateful for the silence though. Making small talk wasn't something she had the strength to do this evening.

'We're not far away now.' Cara glanced at Emma. 'When you can see the ocean, you'll know we've arrived.'

Emma couldn't remember the last time Flora had taken her to the coast. If her heart had still been able to thump in her chest, she was sure it would be skipping a beat. Since she was a child something about the waves had fascinated her, something almost hypnotic. She recalled a documentary she had seen with Flora about the magnetic pull of the moon and the waves, and she marvelled once again at the supernatural lure of the sea.

'There!' Cara nodded at the horizon.

The car rounded a bend in the road, and a smattering of lights twinkled in the bay below them. A few streetlights illuminated the rows of shops and houses that curved around the gaping mouth of the ocean.

They began to descend toward the town. Crossing the bridge in the harbour, Cara turned the car to the east along a tight lane leading up to a clifftop. Almost immediately the ruins appeared ahead of them, silhouetted against the midnight blue of the sky—tall arches, fallen stones, and crumbling towers that framed the magnificent remains of Gothic windows. It was breathtakingly beautiful, even in the darkness. Emma sensed the centuries of stories this iconic building possessed.

'Your exclusive vampire club is at Whitby Abbey?' The irony wasn't lost on her. She had devoured Bram Stoker's novel as a youngster, swept up in the brilliance of the story. 'A bit clichéd, don't you think?'

Cara chuckled. 'It's genius if you think about it. The founders of the Haven were here long before the legends and stories of vampires surrounded this place. The first Haven members still remember Henry VIII sending his men to violate the abbey during the dissolution of the monasteries. It's the perfect hiding place.'

She was right, of course. With the popularity of a myth, anyone visiting the ruins wouldn't think twice about seeing a vampire, fangs and all, strolling through the grounds. They would assume it was a die-hard fan or a fancy-dress costume.

'Besides, the Haven isn't inside the abbey,' Cara continued. 'It's underneath it.'

She pulled the car off the main track and down another winding lane until she came to a stop outside something resembling a fisherman's cottage. A single lamp shone from the downstairs window, splashing a pool of light on the path outside.

'Are they expecting us?' Emma asked, even though she wasn't sure who or what *they* were. Cara had told her the most basic facts about the secret society—they claimed to keep the humans safe from vampire attacks, and the vampires safe from themselves. Beyond that, she was clueless and woefully unprepared.

The door of the cottage swung open, and a huge man with a full grey beard and wild hair filled the space. He was as tall as the door-frame with shoulders that spread out as wide. His faded jeans and knitted jumper had seen better days, but his smile was genuine, as was the sparkle in his eyes.

'Welcome home, Cara. I see you've brought us a new recruit.'

Cara embraced the broad-shouldered man like an old friend before introducing Emma with a flourish of her hand.

'Dustin, this is Emma. She's more than just a new recruit.' Cara winked at her companion.

Dustin raised an eyebrow and looked in Emma's direction. Emma suddenly felt exposed. It reminded her of those times when her teacher made her stand and recite something from a textbook in front of the entire class.

He whistled a long, low sound that carried off toward the sea. 'Wow. I had my doubts when you told me about your mission, but this is incredible. I never thought I'd be the Revenant who got to entertain an Immortal.' He reached forward and pulled Emma into a bear hug. 'Welcome to the Haven, Emma.'

'Thank you,' Emma said, wriggling free of his arms. 'Nice to meet you, I think.'

He laughed throatily and ushered them inside the cottage. Emma followed Cara, keeping Dustin in her peripheral vision. A log fire crackled in the hearth, and a well-worn sofa littered with mismatched pillows sat beneath the window. Piles of books covered every available space. They were stacked up on the coffee table, on the floor, and on the desk in the corner of the room. A black cat stretched and yawned from its position on a folded blanket not far from the fire as it eyed the newcomers who had disturbed its slumber.

'Shall I pop the kettle on?' Dustin didn't wait for an answer. With some difficulty he manoeuvred through a small archway into a tiny kitchen space. The rattle of cups and spoons accompanied the click of the kettle.

'Take a seat, Emma. We'll be here for a short while before we go down to the Haven. Dustin needs to process you.'

'Dustin needs to what?' Emma didn't like the sound of being processed, whatever that meant. She had been through enough the last few days without being prodded and poked by an odd fisherman, even if he seemed kind.

'Don't you worry about that,' Dustin said as he set a tray of steaming mugs and a plate of biscuits on the top of a pile of books. 'We have plenty of time for a drink and a snack before the formalities begin.'

Emma remained standing despite Dustin offering her a seat multiple times. She only became conscious that she was slowly inching toward the door when Cara asked her where she was going.

'There's nothing but cliffs and ruins out there, princess. Why don't we have a chat over a nice cup of tea, and you can ask me anything you want?' Dustin said.

Emma didn't know whether it was his calming voice or the pull toward the chocolate biscuits and the roaring fire that coaxed her to drop onto the sofa and take a sip from the hot, sweet tea. Whatever it was, she started to feel less jumpy and a lot more inquisitive.

'Did you mean it?' She cradled the cup as if the heat might somehow warm her cold, dead hands. 'Can I ask you anything?'

'Shoot.' He dunked his third biscuit into his mug. 'What do you want to know?'

'You called yourself a Revenant earlier. What does that mean?'

'Ah, I hadn't realised I'd done that.' He chuckled to himself. 'I'm usually grislier when Cara brings home a newbie.'

Cara rolled her eyes as if remembering the many moments he was referring to.

Dustin continued, 'In the old days, a Revenant was a kind of vampire servant. They were perpetually hypnotised to do their master's bidding. These days it's more of a mutual alliance.'

'You serve the vampires?'

'Aye, I do. It's the Revenant's job to make sure the Haven and its occupants are safe and that everyone gets what they need.'

'You mean blood?'

'Yes, amongst other things. Providing blood is a small part of my job. I look after the Codex, process the new recruits, ensure that the conditions belowground are as they should be.'

'Do they feed on you?' The same bubbling panic she'd felt when Paul Parker had sat opposite her in the kitchen back home now rose in her stomach. She didn't want to feed on Dustin or any other human.

Dustin laughed again. The booming sound scared the cat, who shot through its flap and off into the night.

'There'd be nowt left of me if I had to feed everyone in the Haven.' He wiped a tear from his eye. 'I might be a big fella, but not even I have enough blood in my veins for two hundred vampires.'

She tried to process what he had said as he dunked yet another biscuit into his mug. Two hundred vampires. *Two hundred.*

'Are you telling me that down there'—she stabbed her finger at the floor for emphasis—'there are two hundred vampires?'

Dustin leaned down to retrieve a large burgundy book from the floor. It crinkled as he turned the pages. 'Yes, here it is. The last entry was a month ago, and he was number 202.'

Dustin thrust the tome into Emma's hands, and her eyes travelled down the list of names on the page. The final inscription was *202—Dale Proctor.* It was written in cursive with a date stamp at the side. Flipping back through the pages revealed names and dates going back to the fifteenth century.

'Have you met all these people?'

'Do I really look that old?' Dustin chuckled again. 'I'm human, princess. I'm one fella in a long line of Revenants tasked with guarding the key and the secrets to the Haven. For generations, we've kept the balance between light and darkness, keeping the humans safe, while making sure the half-bloods don't get into any trouble. None of us want a war. I'm the first point of entry to the Haven, so it's my job to serve at the moment.'

'Do you need to add my name to this list?' It unnerved Emma that her entire existence was about to be reduced to a number, but maybe that was the only reward for death.

'Yes, I'll add you to the pages, but it's so I can remember who everyone is. Think of it as a school register. For you to gain access to the Haven, I'll need to take some of your blood for analysis.'

'Analysis?' Emma narrowed her eyes. 'Cara already told me you know everything about me, so why do you need to analyse me?'

'Cara is right. We know about every vampire out there, but you're an Immortal. We need to double-check that you are who we think you are.'

Cara raised her eyes from the mug she was sipping from long enough to gauge Emma's reaction.

'I've made mistakes before, Emma,' she said. 'I thought I'd found an Immortal years ago, but I was wrong. The vampire in question tricked me and infiltrated the Haven, slaughtering many of my friends in one night.'

'That's awful. I thought all vampires were Immortal by default.'

'We are to a point. Once a half-blood is turned, we can live forever, but we can also be killed by a stake to the heart or drowned in holy water. We learn to use our gifts to avoid being in a situation where that might happen. You, on the other hand, are a true Immortal. You were born a vampire, albeit a dormant one for nearly eighteen years. The only way to kill an Immortal vampire is to behead them and burn their body. Their ashes are then buried in consecrated ground. An Immortal won't explode like a half-blood vampire.'

Dustin ripped the tab off a blood bag and poured the contents into Emma's now empty mug.

'It's a lot to take in, princess. For now, you need to keep your strength up.'

The thought of being beheaded, burned, and buried left a strange ache in Emma's chest. Was being an Immortal hereditary? Were her ancestors now a pile of ash in a random churchyard somewhere? None of it made any sense.

'If I was born a vampire, dormant or not, surely that means my parents would also be vampires, but I know for a fact that my mum died in childbirth.'

'Aye, your mum was as human as they come, but your dad, well, he comes from a long line of vampires.'

Emma's brain reeled at this new information. Was this where the darkness that skirted her soul came from? Could you inherit pain and suffering?

'It's not true,' she whispered. 'My dad was a lawyer and died in a car accident before I was born.'

'Stories told to keep your family line a secret, I'm afraid,' Cara said.

'I don't understand how it's possible. If my father was a vampire, then wouldn't my grandmother have noticed that her son-in-law had fangs?'

'Everything will be revealed in time, princess. Try to keep yourself calm.'

Despite being human, Dustin had clearly picked up on the spike in Emma's anxiety as this new knowledge flooded her brain.

'Do you know who turned me?' she asked instead, hoping to find some scraps of information.

Cara and Dustin exchanged a look, the kind that usually came before an abrupt change of subject or a hasty retreat. Emma jumped in with a follow-up question before either of them could run.

'The person who fed me their blood wasn't the same vampire who attacked me.' She watched their reactions for any slight movement or tension. 'It was a man who bit me, but I think someone else told him to do it.'

'Why do you say that?' Dustin asked.

'He said that someone told him I'd taste as sweet as a summer's day.'

Cara inhaled sharply and jumped up from the sofa.

'I'm sure the Haven's leaders will be able to answer your questions, but we really do need to move on.'

'So, neither of you are going to tell me the truth?'

Again, they exchanged looks.

'I'm sorry, princess. Once Cara has reported in, I'm sure you'll be able to find out more about why you're here. Until then, why not enjoy the ride?'

He drained his tea and flipped open a beautiful wooden box with a large *H* embossed in gold across the top. Curving lines entwined with the letter, stretching out to the four corners of the case and disappearing over the edges. Inside, the lining was a deep red velvet with a row of clear glass test tubes in the lid and an odd-looking contraption in the base.

'It'll only sting for a second,' Dustin said as he lifted a brass gun from the box. He slotted an empty tube to the barrel and moved around the coffee table toward Emma.

On instinct, she held out her arm like the nurse had done to her in hospital before she flinched away from the needle, but Dustin shook his head.

'I need your neck,' he said apologetically.

The needle was fine but still stung as it sank into her skin. The flashback was sudden and frightening. *Fangs, pain, blood, panic.*

'Steady, Emma.' Cara placed her hand on Emma's arm and spoke in a soothing tone in her ear. 'Dustin won't hurt you.'

Emma flipped her gaze to the big man on her other side with his wild hair and grey beard. He winked at her, and her fear subsided, calming her racing thoughts.

'Nearly done,' he said with a warm smile.

There was a small hiss as Dustin disconnected the strange object from Emma's neck and ejected a glass tube full of her blood. He jammed a stopper in the end before securing it in the breast pocket of his jumper.

'I'll be back in a second.' He placed the gun-shaped tool back in the box and left the room.

'You okay, Emma?' Cara's face was expressionless, but her eyes twinkled with concern.

Emma didn't think she would ever be okay again. She was a vampire, her grandmother was missing, she was about to enter a vampire stronghold, and a big man had just run off with a test tube of her blood. What was okay about this situation?

'Yes, I'm fine,' she lied.

Dustin wore a bright smile when he walked back into the room. 'She's good to go! Cara was spot-on. We've got ourselves a true Immortal. Princess, you've got a free pass to the Haven.'

'Thanks,' she mumbled, watching as Cara made her way toward a large bookshelf that filled an entire wall at the end of the living room. She pulled one of the books toward her at an angle and fiddled with something behind it until the entire wall shook and slid forward.

Swinging one end of the gigantic bookshelf open, Cara revealed a heavy metal door. A control panel hung on the wall, and a red light illuminated the back of the shelving unit.

'Dustin, if you please.'

With a grin and a flick of his wrist, Dustin produced a key card from his pocket and swished it along a narrow opening in the control panel. The red light blinked and turned green as a hissing sound filled the room. The metal door inched open, and Emma began to feel the first fluttering of panic. Was she about to be locked in an underground dungeon?

'It's okay, princess. You'll be safe in the Haven, and I'm here to make sure nobody finds you.'

His smile was genuine as he ushered her toward the dark, gaping hole in the wall.

'Why do you keep calling me "princess?"' In truth, it was a stalling strategy on her part, but Dustin had called her "princess" multiple times since their arrival. It suddenly mattered to her.

He didn't appear fazed by her question but merely looked her square in the face.

'Because that's exactly what you are, Emma. A true Immortal, vampire royalty, a princess of darkness.'

4

The ride down to the Haven wasn't quite what Emma had expected. Their mode of transport was a large service elevator with one side full of packing crates. The elevator made a whistling noise as it descended down twenty levels. Finally, the weak bulb above their heads illuminated, informing them of their arrival. The doors opened to reveal a long corridor with windows along both sides. The glass was tinted, so there was no way of knowing who, or what, was on the other side. The raised hairs on Emma's arms and the tingle at the nape of her neck told her that whoever was back there was watching them as they made their journey from the elevator to the main doors.

Cara's long legs carried her down the corridor quickly, and Emma struggled to keep up with her. Her stomach churned the closer they got to the heavy iron doors that marked the entrance to the Haven.

'You okay?' Cara lay her palm flat against a small monitor set back into the wall before glancing back at Emma.

'Never better.' Another lie. Despite the delicious tea Dustin had served them, her mouth was as dry as sandpaper. She couldn't afford to let her nerves get the better of her in this place. There were two hundred vampires behind these big black doors, all with their own unique story and emotional scars. She was about to become just another face, just another girl, just another vampire.

'They'll want to see you straight away, so I'll give you the grand tour later,' Cara continued, obviously taking Emma's lie at face value and moving on.

'Who wants to see me?'

'The council. They are the head of the Haven. All recruiters report to them when a new vamp is brought in. Because you're special, I can't imagine they'll delay meeting you.'

'Recruiters?'

Cara opened the doors, and they walked into a large space with low-voltage lighting strung across the ceiling from wall to wall. The lights sent shadows scuttering into the corners as Cara and Emma moved through the room.

'Recruiters are vampires sent out into the community to round up stray half-bloods and bring them in.'

'What if they don't want to come?'

Cara stopped, and Emma crashed into the back of her with a yelp.

'They don't have a choice. Half-bloods can be unpredictable and dangerous if left to their own devices. The Haven brings them in, trains them, and looks after their needs. Any half-blood who lives outside the Haven also lives outside the vampire law and becomes known as a rogue.'

The hard glint in her eye told Emma not to push her on the matter. It might not be Emma's first choice to join the Haven and live in an underground bunker, but she was haunted by the memory of feeling lost and alone when Flora was taken. She would stay put— for now.

'Got it!' Emma gave Cara a double thumbs-up. 'Go team Haven.'

• • •

A chill coated Emma's skin as she entered the council chamber. It was a dark room carved into the rock with a long wall of windows that exposed the corridor between the lift and the main door. The semicircle of seats facing the tinted glass confirmed Emma's suspicion that she and Cara had been watched as they had entered the Haven.

Emma wondered if the council's sole job was to sit and inspect the two hundred vampires as they came and went.

A tall man with white hair gestured to a single seat placed in the centre of the room, and Emma sat. She was relieved Cara had been allowed to stay in the room. While Emma sensed her life wasn't in danger, apprehension still swirled through her veins.

'You are Emma Hartfield.' It was a statement rather than a question. 'Daughter of Thomas and Charlotte Hartfield.'

Emma studied the council leaders from beneath her lowered lashes. The group consisted of three men and three women, with the white-haired man claiming centre stage. They were old and powerful, a mixed bunch of characters. They were nothing like Emma had expected from the collective leaders of a vampire empire.

The women were almost regal in their appearance, with coiffed hair, tight-fitting bodices, and full skirts, while the men reclined on wingback chairs like kings watching over their court. There wasn't a pair of Converse, piece of denim, or a modern hairstyle amongst them.

The man who had spoken was called Henric, and according to Cara's brief rundown in the lift, he was turned in 1811 when he was only twenty. He still clung to the dated fashion ideals of the nineteenth century. His dark, fitted jacket hugged his slim frame, covering the bloodred waistcoat that matched his trousers. Emma was momentarily reminded of the joy of being able to see her reflection when she caught sight of Henric's jawline reflected in the shine of his riding boots.

'You are the first of your kind to enter the Haven,' Henric continued, breaking into Emma's thoughts. 'We have never met a Dhampir before.'

'A what?'

'A Dhampir. You're the offspring of a human and a vampire and descended from vampire royalty. You were hidden from your Immortal family by your grandmother and raised as a human until the attack triggered your vampire nature.'

Emma bristled under the stares of the council members as she processed his words.

Dustin had been telling her the truth; she *was* a princess. Emma thought back to her childhood. Flora had never had any photos of her parents together. The father who had allegedly died before she was born, and the mother who had died bringing her into this world. Any average family would have at least one photograph of the happy couple in love and eager to start their family.

'That darkness you spoke about—that was your true vampire nature trying to break free,' Cara said.

'Indeed,' Henric said. 'The Hartfield family are renowned for their...darkness.'

Emma didn't miss the hint of sarcasm as it rolled off Henric's tongue, and the nerves fluttering around her stomach multiplied as she glanced at the vampires gathered in front of her.

The darkness she carried around didn't feel like it came from a good place. It had left her consumed by anger and fear, and it had kept her small and broken all these years. If her ancestors were pure darkness, then maybe Cara and her strange Haven would offer her the answers she needed to not only find Flora but also herself.

The council leaders leaned in close to one another and spoke in hushed tones, staring at Emma more than once as their discussion continued. Awareness flooded her senses as she grasped the seriousness of the situation. If the Haven turned her away, she would become what Cara had referred to as a rogue—alone in a dangerous world.

Panic began to bubble in the pit of her stomach, elevating when she sensed someone else watching her from the shadows.

From the way the council seats were arranged, she had assumed Henric was the head of the Haven, but now she was unsure as she watched the silent observer at the edge of the room.

He sat obscured in the dark shadows. A weak circle of light illuminated the council with Emma sitting in the centre and Cara standing off to her left, but this man stayed out of the conversation. His eyes never left Emma as the discussion flowed between the gathered vampires. He didn't look much older than Emma, but despite the fact that no words passed his lips, there was no denying the power that rolled off him.

The pull to look in his direction was magnetic, and she struggled to stop her eyes from wandering more often than was polite. It bugged her that he hadn't spoken, as she wanted so badly to hear the sound of his voice.

'Despite your lineage, we are willing to offer you sanctuary and the resources you need to find your grandmother,' Henric said, breaking through Emma's trance. 'The woman may have information that could be of use to us. Cara, you will supervise this and integrate Emma into your nest.'

'Yes, Henric. May I recommend that Emma join us on our next mission? An early trial to gauge her aptitude and abilities may be useful.'

He glanced around the circle and received a series of nods from everyone gathered. 'Yes, yes, we approve.'

Whatever Cara had signed Emma up for seemed to be a popular option. She, on the other hand, felt the nerves fluttering to life once again. She had been a vampire for only a matter of days. Going on a mission would only confirm a severe *lack* of aptitude and ability.

'I would ask one thing of you, Ms Hartfield.' Henric's voice sliced through her musings. 'Do not reveal your Immortal status to anyone in the Haven other than those assembled here today. Is that clear?'

'Yes, sir.' She didn't know why it mattered, but from the wrinkled brows and tight expressions on the faces of the leaders gathered in the circle, she felt it wise to follow their orders—for now.

A stocky man with thick red hair ushered Emma and Cara out of the dimly lit room and back along the corridor toward a large open space full of people chatting and laughing. To a naive observer, it resembled a college recreation room with sofas grouped around low coffee tables and long tables littered with papers and books. Dartboards dotted one wall and banks of computers were spaced evenly opposite them.

As they approached the entrance, everyone stopped what they were doing and turned toward them.

'Welcome to the Haven,' Cara said with a wide smile.

Unlike the uncomfortable feeling in the coffee shop back in Allendale, the faces here were relaxed and smiling. A few people waved at them in greeting, and they even got a "hey, newbie" from a group of boys playing cards. Emma was relieved to see no one whispering behind their hands or judging her life—or death.

'You belong here, Emma, and I'm going to prove to you how valuable that sense of belonging can be.'

She wondered if Cara had used her vampire sense to tap into any negative vibes she might have been emitting. Her fear of the darkness in her soul tainting her relationships had caused disconnection between herself and the only family she had. The dark void she had created was like a cloak that had wrapped itself around her body and deflected the good, the bad, and the indifferent. It was apparent from watching the people in this room that they shared a bond, but not the same kind that the popular or sporty groups in Allendale had shared. This felt natural, organic, and strangely safe. She still resisted the thought of joining in, but she couldn't deny the peace that had settled over her since stepping into the Haven's inner sanctum.

A small group broke away from the computers and wound their way through the tables and chairs to stand before Cara and Emma. They looked like a poster campaign for an indie band. Dressed head to foot in black, the boys wore dark jeans and faded T-shirts. Their Doc Martens boots were scuffed enough to confirm they participated in plenty of outdoor activities. The girls wore ripped jeans and studded belts with layered tees and heavy eye makeup. They reminded Emma of the yin and yang symbol as they both sported long, straight hair—one jet black and the other platinum blonde.

'Emma, I'd like you to meet my guys.'

She glanced up at Cara for a moment as the pitch in her voice rose ever so slightly. Cara was proud of these people, and it showed. Her smile lit up her entire face as the four newcomers circled them.

'Kai, Jess, Simran, Dylan.' She introduced each in turn as she spoke their name, and they each gave a smile, nod, or salute.

'Nice to meet you,' Emma said, realising she meant it. Before Cara had arrived at her door, the only experience she'd had with vampires was violent, bloody, and deadly.

The boy called Dylan thrust his hand out for Emma to shake. His teeth were ever so slightly crooked as he grinned at her and winked. 'Glad to have you in the nest, Emma.'

She flinched at his words and focused on Cara.

'Nest? Really?'

Dylan chuckled and slid his arm around Emma, steering her out of the recreation room and along the corridor.

'It's not as dodgy as it sounds, Em. Can I call you "Em?"' He didn't wait for her answer. 'Think of it as a term of endearment from our gang. Everyone in the Haven is divided into groups, or families if you like, and that's what the word *nest* stands for. You're part of our family now.'

An odd feeling flooded her chest, and she realised with a start that she was fighting back tears that threatened to fall. In one brief interaction, Dylan had hit upon her main weakness—family. Flora was far from perfect, but she was all Emma had in the world. The feeling of loss was almost too much to bear.

'Dylan is right.' Simran slipped her arm through Emma's other arm and fell into step beside them. Her silky black hair swished as they walked. 'Cara's nest is one of the best. In fact, you can call us "the elite."' She laughed, and it was like a musical melody. Her slim frame shook as her giggles continued until they reached the double doors that separated the sleeping quarters from the living quarters.

'What makes you elite?' Emma asked, growing curious about this small group of strangers who walked, talked, and flowed in perfect synchronicity.

'We've been on more topside missions than any other nest in the Haven, and we've banked the most new vamps for the ranks.' Kai spoke with passion and pride about their collective achievements, and the high fives and fist bumps from his friends mirrored this.

They were a tight-knit unit. Despite all of Cara's grand talk and promises, Emma couldn't see how she would be able to integrate into this group, even with the orders Henric and the Haven had given.

They strode through the double doors and entered a hallway resembling an apartment block. A row of numbered doors ran the full length of the corridor. Dylan and Simran pulled them to a stop outside a dark grey door with the number seven on it.

'Welcome to the nest,' Dylan said as he turned the handle and shoved the door open.

The recreation area had wowed Emma, but this was something else. It was like stepping into one of those glossy home décor magazines. The walls were painted a warm cream with a deep navy feature wall at the far end of the room.

Two large grey sofas with an assortment of coloured throws and cushions stood in the centre of the space, facing a glass coffee table covered in magazines and coffee cups.

Bookshelves loaded with books, vinyl albums, and potted plants lined the walls. The corner closest to the front door housed a small kitchen area and a breakfast bar where Kai now sat watching her reaction with obvious delight.

'Were you expecting coffins?'

She laughed, but her cheeks burned. He was right; coffins were precisely what she had been expecting. So much for no stereotyping.

'When Cara told me you all lived in an underground bunker, I wasn't quite sure what to expect. It was a toss-up between coffins or hammocks.'

'You'd never get me in either,' said Jess as she motioned for Emma to follow her to one of the doors off the living space. 'This is the girls' room, and that's where the boys sleep.' She pointed at the door on the opposite wall. 'Cara is in the one opposite the kitchen.'

Emma nodded, taking it all in. The apartment was beautiful and inviting, but it gave her a sudden burst of homesickness for her tired green room back at Flora's house.

'We made room for you,' Jess added as she ushered her into the bedroom.

Three of the walls were painted red, and maps, photographs, and posters covered the fourth. Three single beds lined the longest section of the wall, each with a small set of drawers separating them.

'That's your bed.' Simran gestured to the one nearest the door with a pile of clean bedding and towels on the end. 'You've also got space in the wardrobe for anything you need to hang, not that we get to wear dresses here.'

Her eyes twinkled as she spoke, and Emma knew Simran was happy about that. She couldn't imagine either girl wearing some of the dresses the Allendale population wore.

'Shall we get to work?' Cara's voice broke into her thoughts.

'Let's find your grandmother,' Jess said with a wink. 'Time for your first mission!'

• • •

Simran hadn't been joking when she said the vampires from Cara's nest were elite. Everywhere the group went within the bunker they attracted a crowd. Simran and Dylan lapped up the attention, while Jess and Kai remained one step away, assessing their surroundings and observing the interactions. It only took Emma a few nights in the Haven to notice how they worked together as a group. She quickly started to piece together their pattern.

To an untrained eye, Simran and Dylan were fun-loving vampires who joined the crowd, knew everyone's name, and appeared almost flighty in their encounters with the other nests. They talked, laughed, and wound their way through the gathered groups like water around a well-caressed boulder.

Simran's flawless skin and inky black hair, teamed with her authenticity and magnetic smile, drew the other vampires to her like bees to a hive. Her laughter hypnotised them to the extent that they divulged all their secrets. Emma found herself just as mesmerised as she watched from her safe spot on the sofa in the darkest corner of the room.

A velvety voice interrupted her musings.

'You'll never make any friends if you keep skulking in the shadows.'

Emma was startled to find herself gazing into the eyes of the silent vampire from her initial meeting with Henric and the council.

He smiled, causing the tiny creases around his eyes to bunch up. She had assumed he was not much older than she was, but upon closer inspection, he was probably closer to his early twenties in human years. As a vampire, he radiated age and experience that were impossible for Emma to comprehend.

'How are you finding life at the Haven?'

The simple fact that she'd only met with the council a few days earlier meant that "life" at the Haven was yet to be established, but what Emma had seen so far wasn't altogether displeasing.

'It's all very new. I'm still adjusting to becoming a vampire let alone living in a secret underground bunker.'

His laugh lit up his entire face. In a fashion throwback to the vampires of Emma's favourite books and movies, his hair remained long and was secured neatly at the nape of his neck. Even though he listened and spoke to her, his gaze drifted to the room like an ever-vigilant head teacher.

'So, are you one of the leaders of the Haven?' A rising need to know everything about this man drove Emma to break her cardinal rule of staying silent and invisible.

'I hold a position of authority, yes.'

He offered nothing more, and frustration bubbled up in Emma's chest. She was the one who was standoffish and mysterious. It was new territory to be the one eager to push for answers.

'How does it work then? Do we call you "sir" as if we were in school, or do we use Christian names like those hip professors I've read about?'

He swung to face her and extended his hand. Instinctively, she slipped her palm into his, feeling the coolness of his touch. The rough skin on his palms told her he wasn't a stranger to manual labour.

'You can call me James.'

'I'm Emma.' She didn't care that he already knew who she was.

James's gaze searched her face, skimming over her lips, before settling on her eyes. Emma couldn't tear herself away from his scrutiny. His eyes were the deepest blue, almost navy, with a perfect rim of red around the iris. He released her hand, placing his own over his chest and giving her a small bow.

'I hope you settle in well, Emma, and I wish you luck in finding your grandmother.'

With that, he spun away and sauntered off into the crowd, slipping through the hustle and bustle as though he were an apparition. Nobody acknowledged him as he walked, and Emma began to wonder if she had dreamt him up.

'You okay?' Dylan flopped into the seat next to Emma, his curly hair dancing around his face as he wriggled to get comfortable.

'I want to find Flora.' She pushed her interaction with James to the back of her mind.

'Don't worry. As soon as the sun sets, we'll go topside and start hunting.'

Emma's nose wrinkled at his choice of words. Was this what her life had become—one long hunt for people, answers, and blood?

'Where do we even start? My grandmother was taken from Allendale. Surely any clues will be back there.'

'No need to retrace your steps. We have sources here in the Haven that can find anybody—human or vampire.'

'Sources?'

Kai joined them and straddled the chair opposite Emma, resting his large boot on the edge of the sofa.

'There's a network of vampires across the country who share intel,' Kai added. 'If vamps took your grandmother, then someone will know about it. We've just got to find the right links.'

'I thought the Haven had rounded up all vampires under one roof?' Emma said.

'Can you imagine that?' Dylan burst out laughing and playfully punched Emma's arm. 'Isn't this party big enough for you, Em?'

She giggled at his boyish glee.

'There are way more than two hundred vampires in the country,' Kai said. 'The Haven registers every half-blood, but it isn't home to them all. Think of this as the headquarters of a global corporation.'

'Oh. So your sources are part of the Haven but aren't here in the bunker?'

'Yes, there are nests that live on the road. They travel the country and keep the peace. A bit like vampire sheriffs!'

Emma chuckled at Kai's description. He was obviously popular here at the Haven, judging by the glances he got as he moved through the bunker, but Kai was the quietest of Cara's group. He was the silent observer, and Emma felt an instant connection to him. Where Dylan and Simran were the life of the party, Kai was the soul.

'Do you think they'll be able to find a lead to Flora's whereabouts?'

'Absolutely! There's nowhere to hide from the Haven.'

A slight chill ran down Emma's spine at his words. She felt comfortable now, but would that change over time? Once the nest located Flora, would the council let her leave with her grandmother, or would they make her say goodbye to the only family she had ever known? She locked these questions away in her brain for later. Perhaps Dustin could shed some light on them when the time came. As the only human in the vicinity, he would be a useful ally.

Simran's laughter carried across the hall and pulled Emma's attention from her silent musing.

'She's got the deadliest weapon of us all.' Kai looked over his shoulder to smile at his friend.

'What do you mean?'

'All of us have a special gift of some kind,' Kai said. 'Mine is related to the senses, but Simran's gift is like a siren's.'

'A siren? You mean the girls who lured sailors to the rocks with their songs and drowned them?'

'Yeah, except our Sim doesn't have to sing to hypnotise her prey. She only has to utter a few words, and they're vampire bait.'

Emma studied the girl through fresh eyes, and for the first time, she noticed the dazed expressions on the faces of the young men and women surrounding her. They hung on to her every word, soaking up her energy and vying for her attention.

'Do I have a gift?'

'We all do,' Kai said. 'You just have to work out what it is. Sometimes you'll have a sense of it, but generally, it develops over time. Sim was so popular when she first arrived at the Haven that Henric had to get involved and explain her gift to her.'

'She hypnotised one of the oldest vampires in here.' Dylan laughed loudly and slapped his hand on his thigh. 'You should have seen the look on the old guy's face when he realised Sim had manipulated him into giving her a weapons allowance!'

Emma laughed with Dylan, feeling a whole new appreciation for her roommate.

'Your gift will emerge in time,' Kai said. 'You can't force it. You can only watch out for things you excel at.'

'Well, I don't think I'll have Simran's talents.' Emma nodded toward the girl holding court in the centre of the hall. 'It's more likely I'll show an exceptional talent for clumsiness or something equally useless.'

Dylan slid his arm around Emma. 'Whatever your talent is, Em, you'll rock it. If it's falling over your own feet, then you'll be the best at it.' He laughed and squeezed her shoulder. Emma swatted him away with a giggle.

'What are you guys talking about?' Simran stood over them with her hands tucked into her jean pockets.

They doubled over with laughter, and Simran good-humouredly slapped both boys around the back of the head.

'Have you been talking about me?' Simran asked.

'It was all good,' Emma said. 'We were trying to figure out what my vampire talent might be, and they told me about your gift.'

'Honey, you're going to have the coolest of talents. I feel it in my bones,' Simran said.

'I hope so.'

'Heads up, guys.' Dylan's smile vanished from his face.

Emma followed his line of sight and spotted Jess storming through the crowd toward them. Her eyes blazed red, and her platinum blonde hair swung violently behind her.

'If I ever say I'm ready for a real relationship again, will one of you lock me away?' Jess dropped onto the sofa next to Dylan.

'Who upset you this time?' Dylan asked.

'Katie! The backstabbing bitch told me we were exclusive, and then I found out that she's been seeing someone from Pierce's nest too.'

Emma sat back and watched her new comrades as they consoled their friend and swore to freeze out Katie. Slowly, they pulled Jess out of the darkness and back into the light. Emma had never had anyone she trusted enough to be that open and honest with. No friends or relationships to call her own.

Cara's group had welcomed her with open arms, and for that, she would be eternally grateful.

It seemed strange to think this tight-knit unit might offer her everything she had ever wanted—a family.

5

Cara had sent her team into the recreation hall with strict instructions to listen for whispers of information that might lead to Flora's whereabouts. After sunset, they would be going topside to start their mission. While they waited for sunset, Cara, Kai, Dylan, Sim, and Jess retired to room seven and slept.

Still running on a human schedule, sleep evaded Emma. She listened for the soft sounds of breathing or the occasional snore, but the girls remained silent—death had stolen their most natural elements. It unnerved Emma more than she wanted to admit.

Swinging her legs out of bed, Emma pulled on joggers and a T-shirt. She slipped into her sneakers and headed out into the corridor. Surely someone would be awake in the bunker, a solitary night owl—or would that be day owl in the vampire world?

The corridors were silent, and the recreation room was encased in darkness. It resembled an abandoned building from the postapocalyptic movies she used to watch. In the far corner of the hall, a single computer screen cast its milky glow over a tiny circle of space, and Emma felt the hypnotic pull of her human side craving the light.

The soft hum of the hard drive was a small comfort as Emma slipped into the vacant seat at the computer. A black-and-white photograph of a large manor house filled the screen. It was an imposing building with two three-story turrets on either side of the main doors. The drive swept up a small incline bordered by manicured lawns and flower beds. It was beautiful and haunting.

Emma scrolled down the page until she came across the description. Her fingers hovered over the mouse as she spotted the name of the building. *Hartfield Manor*. It was the centuries-old residence of Edward Hartfield, a well-known philanthropist who had died in tragic circumstances. The estate had been left to his two sons, Victor and Thomas Hartfield.

If her heart could beat, Emma was confident it would have been breaking free of her chest. Was this a strange coincidence, or was someone toying with her? Flora had spent hours telling Emma about her parents. Even though most of it had been lies, she did recall the story about her mother marrying Thomas Hartfield at his family estate. She had loved listening to the tales of how they had met and fallen in love. It had been a way to feel close to the mum and dad she'd never known.

Was this her father's home? Flora had told her he was from Yorkshire, but that was a large county. Surely there were many Hartfields in the area. If she had stumbled across this information in the comfort of her bedroom back in Allendale, it wouldn't have freaked her out so much. But as she sat in the dark recreation hall of a vampire bunker, it seemed too much of a coincidence for her to have discovered this by accident.

She glanced behind her. Her eyes adjusted to the black room, but she didn't see anybody stirring in the shadows. Someone was watching her though; it felt like a soft caress over her skin. She could not sense precisely where they were though.

Henric had made her swear to keep her lineage a secret, yet it was clear someone had wanted her to discover this.

Turning her attention back to the screen, she continued scrolling through the page. There was more information about the architecture of the building, the extensive grounds, and lake house, as well as more black-and-white photographs. Nothing on the site was up-to-date information. Instead, it read like an encyclopaedia page on Wikipedia.

All the statistics were from an archive, and when Emma clicked on the link, a pop-up appeared asking for her Haven login information.

'Is everything okay?' James emerged from the darkness, startling Emma. She quickly flicked the screen off to hide what she'd been looking at.

'Insomnia. Guess I'm still running on a human body clock.'

'You shouldn't be wandering the halls, Emma. If the guards find you out here after hours, you might get in trouble.'

'Guards? Nobody told me about any guards!' Was that whom she had sensed watching her—a lone guard keeping an eye on the newbie vampire? Or was it James's presence she had detected?

'Henric assigned guards to monitor the bunker during our sleep period after an attack some years ago. It's for our safety. If they see you out of bed, they might be inclined to stake first and ask questions later.' He winked at her, and Emma was grateful she could no longer blush. 'Allow me to escort you back to your room.'

She followed James through the halls. Her skin tingled every time his hand bumped against hers. Hoping to distract herself from his close proximity, she decided to use the opportunity to find out more about her ancestors.

'What do you know about the Immortal families?'

James inhaled deeply, and she thought he was about to reprimand her for asking the question. Instead, he stopped walking and cleared his throat.

'They're old. Older than anyone can comprehend. Over hundreds of years, the Immortal families destroyed entire towns before they discovered they could feed on humans without killing them.'

Emma shivered.

'Some of the Immortals understood how special their blood was and began turning humans into weaker versions of themselves—the half-bloods they now despise.'

'So, the Haven is here to keep half-bloods safe from humans *and* the Immortals?'

'Yes, that's right. Keeping you safe is our top priority.'

She wished he meant her specifically, but she knew James was referring to the Haven as a whole.

'Do you feel safe?' He leaned in as he spoke.

Emma held her breath. All thought escaped her as she pressed her back against the wall. She nibbled at her lower lip as he came closer, but he reached around her and opened the door to number seven.

She knew her cheeks remained pale, but an almost overwhelming heat rushed through her. He wasn't going to kiss her; he was merely opening the door.

'Yes,' she whispered. 'I feel safe.'

He smiled and brought her hand to his lips, pressing them to her skin, before disappearing down the corridor. Emma let out the breath she had been holding and giggled. James was a council leader, but she couldn't shake her giddiness.

This time, when she snuggled between the sheets, her sleep was laced with dreams of big empty rooms, long-lost fathers, and handsome vampires in the darkness.

• • •

The buzzer tore through Emma's dreams like an out-of-control school bell, pulling her away from the endless darkness where she searched for answers.

'Morning, sleepyhead.' Simran's smiling face leaned over the bed. 'That lovely sound you hear is your alarm clock for the rest of time.' She laughed and pulled her jumper over her head, shaking her long hair out and scraping it back into a tight ponytail.

'How can you be so damn cheerful in the morning—I mean, evening?' Emma crawled out of bed and rubbed her face as if the movement might force her eyes to work and her brain to fire up.

'She's had centuries of training!' Jess winked as she left the bedroom with her overly cheerful friend in tow, grabbing their jackets on the way. 'Meet you at the briefing centre in five.'

Emma muttered under her breath as she washed and dressed. Being a vampire had to be a conspiracy against young adults and their desire to sleep long, uninterrupted hours.

The briefing centre was, in fact, a lecture theatre with rows of tiered seating. A large screen dominated the front of the space where two women stood addressing the gathered groups. Jess waved Emma over as she entered the room, and Emma hurried to join her nest.

One of the women began speaking, referring to the files on the table in front of her. 'Pierce, your group is on recon. We've had reports of a rogue nest in Leeds. They need to be brought in or eliminated. Use your discretion.'

A thin man with slicked-back hair and a moustache nodded at the speaker. The six vampires surrounding him grinned as if they had been told they'd won an all-expenses-paid trip to Disneyland.

Jess sucked in a sharp breath, and Simran instinctively grabbed her hand. Emma cast another look over at the group and recognised Katie in the middle. She was petite compared to the others, almost doll-sized. Her small frame was mostly hidden from view by a woman with bright red hair who cradled Katie like a protected ward. Judging by Jess's reaction, Emma assumed this was the new relationship that had hurt her so much.

From the authoritative way the redhead smothered Katie, Emma wasn't sure Katie was happy with her new girlfriend. By observing the daily dramas of Allendale High, Emma had fine-tuned her radar when it came to spotting people doing what was expected rather than what they truly wanted.

The woman began speaking again. 'Cara, your group will travel to the moors and speak to your source about the missing human. She needs to be located and brought immediately to Henric for evaluation.'

Cara bobbed her head in agreement as the rest of them shuffled in their seats. Emma processed what the woman had said. There was no need to bring Flora inside the bunker. Two hundred vampires lived here!

'You have your assignments,' the woman said to the entire room. 'Dismissed.'

The room began to clear, and Emma followed Simran and Jess as they exited the centre.

'Why does my grandmother need to be evaluated?' Emma asked Cara, grabbing her arm as they left the theatre.

'Henric's orders. He has his reasons, and it's not for us to question.'

Emma flinched at the harshness in Cara's tone.

Dylan nudged Emma's elbow. 'The gals in operations take their orders directly from the top. We do as we're told.'

'I don't understand why Flora is of any interest to the Haven. Henric might be the top dog, but that doesn't explain why he needs to evaluate my family.'

'Fair enough.' Dylan tucked his hands into his pockets, and Emma felt a pang of guilt for being so snappy. She knew he was only trying to be supportive.

'I'm sorry, this is all so new to me. It's like I'm being pulled in two.'

'Human versus vampire?'

'Yeah, something like that.'

'It'll get easier, Em. I promise. Hopefully, we'll get you some answers on the moors tonight.'

'When you say moors, do you mean *the* moors?'

Dylan laughed.

'You've seen *An American Werewolf in London* then.'

'Only about twenty times!'

'Don't worry, werewolves aren't real. I'd stay away from the Slaughtered Lamb Pub just to be safe though.' He jumped away from Emma's playful slap. 'Besides, anyone stupid enough to go out on the moors at night deserves to be terrorised by five—sorry, *six* badass vampires.'

Emma followed Dylan as he jogged to catch up to the rest of Cara's nest. She had never thought she would be spending a grey night on the Yorkshire Moors. It should have been a terrifying prospect, but Emma felt the stirrings of excitement for her first mission. If this was her life now, then she had to embrace what that might entail. Once Flora was safe and sound, she could decide what the future held. For now, she planned to throw herself into learning how to be a vampire.

'It's the perfect time to start your training, Emma,' Cara said as the lift carried them up toward Dustin's cottage and the outside world. 'I told Henric I would put you through a trial to ascertain your aptitude and abilities, and there's no better time than tonight.'

'What do you need me to do?' Emma's voice wobbled as her brain worked overtime, running through the possibilities of what this trial might involve. Was Cara about to go all *Hunger Games* on her, or was it more civilised than that?

'When we get to the moors, I want you to take point.'

'Lead your mission?'

'Find and question our source and keep your senses alert for any threats to the team. That's it.'

It sounded easy in principle, but they were dealing with vampires. Her experience prior to arriving at the Haven had been a deadly one.

'I'll try my best.' Emma prayed that her ability was not enhanced clumsiness, and that her aptitude was sniffing out answers.

Dustin was waiting with a warm hug for each of them when they arrived at the top. He was like the favourite uncle you loved to visit.

'I'm online so radio in if you need backup.' Dustin gave Emma a wink. 'I'm not going to let our princess get into any trouble.'

'Princess?' Kai glanced between Dustin and Emma. 'How come I didn't get a nickname?'

'Oh, you did, but I can't repeat it in front of the ladies.' Dustin slapped a big hand on Kai's back and laughed. Emma loved the sound of his laughter, and the subtle booming of his heart that accompanied it.

'Funny.' Kai laughed as he made his way out the front door. 'Now I remember why I prefer to stay below the ground!'

Emma smiled at the group's banter. Dustin was as much a part of their world as any of the vampires in the bunker. He oozed confidence and calm around a species that had the potential to kill him.

'Stay in touch.' Dustin closed the cottage door, and the blackness of the night enveloped them.

• • •

Emma wasn't sure what to expect from the vampire nests that lived out on the moors. Would they be more feral like the man who had mind-warped Paul before attacking her, or would they follow the same rules as the Haven?

'Have you figured out your vamp superpower yet?' Simran asked, interrupting Emma's thoughts. Simran sat in the front passenger seat next to Cara and swivelled to look back at the four of them squashed into the back seat of the car.

Emma glanced at the expectant faces staring at her and rolled her eyes.

'Not yet.' She laughed. 'I only found out about vampire powers recently, so I might need a bit more time to figure it all out.'

'Ticktock,' Simran said. An amused smile danced across her face. 'The sooner you work it out, the more fun you'll have.'

'Don't we all have vampire speed and hypnotic charms?' Emma asked.

'You need to read some new books, Em.' Dylan laughed. 'I'm the only vampire in this car with the speed gene.'

Kai and Jess groaned as Simran burst out laughing.

'You tell 'em, Dylan,' Simran said.

'You mean we're not all as fast as the speed of sound?' Emma asked.

'Nope, that talent was gifted to yours truly.' Dylan puffed his chest out and winked at Emma. 'You guys might be more streamlined than you were as humans, but I'm the vampire you need when you've only got a few seconds to get the job done.'

'What about you?' Emma asked Jess.

'I can see auras,' Jess said. 'It might not be as good as Dylan's power, but I can tell you if someone is lying, scared, angry, or sad from the colour of their aura.'

'That's pretty cool.' Emma wondered what story her aura might tell. She made a mental note to ask Jess when they were alone. 'Kai, what's your superpower?'

Kai's pale face turned toward Emma as the car fell silent. Emma worried that he hadn't heard her, but then she realised she couldn't hear anything at all. No sound whatsoever emanated from the car or its inhabitants.

'What the hell?' Even Emma's words disappeared as she said them.

Like a bubble bursting, the noise whooshed back to her ears, and everyone laughed.

'What was that?' Emma asked.

'I can manipulate your senses,' Kai said. 'I can distort sound, sight, and touch. Make you think you're seeing or hearing something that isn't there.'

Emma said, 'That's amazing.'

'You must have some idea what your power might be, Em.' Dylan nudged her elbow. 'Come on. Spill.'

'Well, I don't know if it's a power, but I can sense when people I can't see are around me.'

'You mean like a stalker hiding behind a wall?' Dylan asked.

'Yes, I guess so,' Emma said. 'I can feel it under my skin, like an itch or something.'

Simran grinned. Her eyes sparkled in the moonlight that shone through the sunroof.

'That's definitely a gift, and I think it's a perfect superpower,' Simran said.

'What do you mean?' asked Emma.

'The sources we have out on the moors aren't always legitimate nests.' Simran glanced at Cara before saying more. 'Some of them are rogue vampires. We get vital information in exchange for not reporting them to the Haven.'

Emma gazed at the faces of her new friends. Simran had shared a secret with her that could get Cara and her entire nest in huge trouble. Rogue vampires weren't tolerated. Pierce's nest was on a mission to terminate a group in Leeds tonight.

'I see. Do you think I'll be able to sense where they are if they're hidden?' asked Emma.

'It's worth a try,' Simran said.

They had trusted her with this information, and a wave of contentment washed over Emma as she focused on the vast expanses of moorland beyond the car window. They settled into a comfortable silence as Cara navigated the car down dark lanes.

'We're here.' Cara's voice broke the quiet, and everyone roused themselves. 'There's a small farmhouse over that hill where rogues have been known to shelter.'

They spilled out of the car. Emma stretched her limbs and let her eyes adjust to the night. With no streetlights around, the moors were cloaked in darkness.

'Emma, what are your orders?' Cara stood ahead of the group; her face turned toward the span of nothing that stretched out before them. The clouds drifted across the fullness of the moon, casting shadows over her assembled friends.

Pressure rose in Emma's chest at the thought of being front and centre. As she looked at the faces of her new friends, she knew they trusted her judgement even though she had no clue what she was doing.

'Relax into it.' Simran stepped forward to take hold of Emma's hands. 'Let your senses relax and see what bubbles up.'

Emma wondered briefly if Simran was using her siren powers on her as the fluttering panic subsided and she started to feel more grounded.

She took a tentative step into the darkness and then another. With her chin lifted, the cool night breeze caressed her cheeks, carrying with it the smell of wood burning.

'I can detect a person. That way.' Emma gestured across the moors toward the north, and the group set off as one.

Swathes of heather littered the ground, making the surface uneven. With the moon hidden behind grey clouds, they had to tap into their vampire reflexes to stay upright. Cara and Kai hung to the back of the group as Emma and Dylan took point. Jess and Simran monitored their flank.

'Stop!' Emma halted and dropped into a crouch. The others followed her lead. 'Someone is watching us.'

'Which direction?' Dylan asked.

'To our left. I can feel their eyes on us.'

'Want me to check it out?' Dylan winked, and Emma recalled the earlier conversation in the car about his speed.

'Yes, see if you can spot anyone.'

In less than the blink of an eye, Dylan was gone. His tangy soap scent lingered in the air. Emma didn't even have time to gasp before he returned clutching a ragged-looking vampire by his jacket.

'Hey, Joey.' Jess stood up and smiled at Dylan's prize.

'Seriously, don't you guys ever use the phone?' Joey asked.

Everyone relaxed as the pale, dirty creature now hemmed inside their wall of bodies greeted them.

Simran giggled and threw her arms around the newcomer's neck. 'It's good to see you, Joey.'

'Yeah, you too, Sim.' His eyes moved from face-to-face, giving a quick smile or nod as he registered each member of the group. When he got to Emma, he stopped and stood a little taller. 'You're new!'

Emma raised her hand in a half wave before realising how ridiculous she must look.

'I'm Emma, a new member of Cara's nest.'

'Cool! Welcome to the crew.' With the pleasantries over, he turned to Dylan. 'How did you find me so fast? I masked my scent with cow's urine—don't ask!'

'Ew, Joey, that's nasty! I can't believe I hugged you.' Simran brushed herself down.

'Our newbie's superpower,' Dylan answered. 'She knew you were watching us.'

'Whoa, that's a nifty gift.' Joey grinned at Emma. 'You'd come in pretty handy on a raid.'

'No!' Cara stepped forward and took control of the moment.

Joey shrank backwards a fraction. Was it on Cara's good graces that this feral vampire wasn't Haven fodder?

'We're looking for information about a human snatched by vampires,' Cara said.

'Ain't that an everyday occurrence for you guys?'

'This human is…important to the Haven. She'll be a prisoner rather than lunch,' Cara replied.

Emma glanced up at Cara, but her face was devoid of any emotion. If the Haven thought Flora was important enough to send their elite nest out looking for her, then she didn't think it would be this easy to find her.

'She's an older lady with wavy grey hair.' Emma hoped the description might jog Joey's memory.

He stared at Emma for a long time before answering. 'Yeah, I think I know who you're talking about.'

'Was she alive?' Kai asked.

Emma turned away with a hitch in her breath. She had been so wrapped up in finding Flora that she hadn't even considered the possibility that Flora might be dead. She spun back toward Joey, awaiting his reply.

'She was when I saw them, although she looked a little banged up. It was sundown when they swept through. They had a car with blacked-out windows. I guess the driver didn't want anyone to know what he was transporting.'

Emma swallowed hard at the thought of her grandmother being beaten.

'How did you see her if the windows were blacked out?' Emma asked.

'That's my gift, sweetheart. I can see through anything reflective. Covered windows, frosted glass, mirrors.'

'Who was in the car?' Cara asked.

'Your old girl and a vamp goon were in the back. The driver and a hooded guard were up front,' Joey said.

'Where were they going?' Emma's voice quivered. Her desperation was seeping into her questions. The sharp memory of the hooded figure crouched over her in the dark alley pushed into her thoughts. Had Flora's fate already been decided?

'From the make and model of the car, there's only one place they could have been going,' Joey said, his jaw tight. 'Hartfield Manor.'

Emma sucked in a breath as Kai threw his hands in the air.

'There's no way we're getting inside that place.' Kai ran his fingers through his hair. 'It's a fortress.'

'Henric might know a way inside,' Jess said with a shrug.

'We can scout the perimeter and look for weaknesses,' Simran added.

Cara locked eyes with Emma as the others offered up solutions to their predicament. In her head, Emma heard the faint whispering of Cara's voice. *'We need to tell them. They need to know that you're a Hartfield.'*

Emma nodded.

'Thank you for the information, Joey,' Cara said. 'We'll take it from here.'

'No problem. I'm always happy to help my buddies.'

Joey said his goodbyes and trudged off into the inky blackness of the moors.

'Will he be okay?' Emma asked, suddenly anxious that the small vampire might be vulnerable on his own.

'Joey will be fine,' Dylan said as he settled into the car beside her. 'There are five rogue vamps out here, and they look out for each other. It's like they've got a nest of their own.'

'Even though they're feral, they have each other's back. Joey and the others keep an eye out for unusual activity and any nests that cross the moors, and they report what they see to Cara. We keep them relatively safe in exchange,' Kai told her.

Emma turned her face toward the car window. The sky was black, yet she could still sense Joey watching them as they drove away.

'What are we going to do about Hartfield Manor?' It was Jess who broached the subject as the car manoeuvred down the lane.

'Can I ask a question?' Emma wasn't sure she wanted to know the answer, but she asked anyway. 'What's so bad about Hartfield Manor?'

Someone in the Haven had wanted her to know about Hartfield Manor. Otherwise, the computer screen displaying the history of the house wouldn't have been left for her to find. Henric had called her a Dhampir—the child of a human mother and a vampire father. Her father was a Hartfield. She was a Hartfield. That meant something. She needed to know what it meant and why it mattered.

'Think of the worst vampire family in existence and then triple the amount of cruelty. Only then will you be able to guess what the Hartfield vampires are like.' Simran's voice floated back from the passenger seat.

'The Haven was created to keep half-blood vampires and humans safe, but the Hartfields are an Immortal family. They despise us. They want us wiped off the face of the earth, and they don't care how they do it,' Dylan said.

Emma caught Cara's gaze in the rearview mirror.

'What I don't understand is how you and your grandmother are involved,' Kai said. 'I get that you're another half-blood they want to destroy, but why take the old lady?'

'If they took Flora, then maybe they're starting to perform human sacrifices.' Dylan scratched his head as if it would help him sort through his thoughts. 'Or could they be using your grandmother as bait to lure us out?'

'You might be right about that,' Cara said suddenly, and Emma's chest tightened in anticipation. The second Cara told them the truth it would be over. No more new friends, no more nest, and no more family. Once they knew who she was, they would reject her.

'I don't think they're using Flora to lure us out of hiding,' Cara said, 'but I think they're hoping it will flush Emma out.'

Everyone in the car turned to look at Emma, confusion etched across their brows.

'How come?' Dylan was the one to ask.

Cara's eyes remained on the road, leaving the question hanging in the air.

'Because I'm a Hartfield,' Emma whispered.

6

Emma felt like an apparition floating aimlessly, longing to be let back into life. The group drove home in silence. The truth was out, and each member of Cara's nest appeared to be processing what they had just learned—Emma Hartfield was the enemy.

Dylan kept his head down. His eyes were trained on his hands folded in his lap. Simran stared out of the front window all the way back to the Haven. Jess and Kai turned away from Emma as the countryside flew past the window.

The gaping wound in Emma's chest was painful. In a matter of days, she had secured her footing inside their world. Yes, she still had more to learn, but there had been the promise of a guiding hand, a supportive shoulder, and a hope that all was not lost. She didn't have to be alone again. All that was now in jeopardy because of who she was—or rather, who her real family was.

Dustin's cottage crept into view, and Kai let out a humourless laugh.

'Princess!' Kai said quietly. 'Now I understand the nickname.'

'I'm sorry,' Emma said. 'I had no idea until Henric told me who my father really was. Flora had told me he was a lawyer from Yorkshire who died before I was born.'

Kai and Jess climbed out of the car and barrelled straight into the cottage. Simran half-smiled and shrugged before following her friends. Dylan stayed in the car, rooted to the back seat.

'I was told not to tell you,' Emma said. 'Henric made me swear to keep it a secret.'

Dylan raised his head to look at her. 'Yes, from everyone else. Not from your own nest. That's a low blow, Em.'

He moved away from her and jumped out of the opposite door. His broad shoulders shoved the cottage door open, and he was swallowed up by the soft lamplight.

'What am I supposed to do now?' Emma asked as she slammed the car door and turned to Cara.

'They'll come around. It'll take time. Opening up about yourself a bit more and letting them in would help.'

'How can I open up when *I* don't even know who the hell I am?'

'I'll see if I can arrange a meeting with James. He might be able to help unlock any hidden memories.'

Emma jumped to attention at the mention of the mysterious vampire leader.

'How can he help me?'

'James is one of the oldest vampires at the Haven, and although on the outside it looks like Henric is in charge, it's James who is the true head of the Haven.' Cara turned toward the cottage. 'His gifts have evolved over the centuries and include tapping into memories. He uses regression techniques to open the mind.'

'Isn't that dangerous?'

'It can't be any worse than dying and becoming a vampire.'

Dustin was waiting for them as they entered the small living space. The cat ignored the interruption and curled up in front of the fire as the big man set a tray of steaming teacups on the table. The others were nowhere to be seen, but the entrance to the elevator was open and the gentle hum of the descending cage filled the air.

'They went on ahead.' Dustin smiled warmly. 'Thought you girls might want a cuppa while you wait for the cage to return.'

Cara flopped onto the sofa and stretched her long legs out in front of her. She caught a section of her hair and twirled it around her finger. Emma perched on the edge of the armchair and gratefully reached for a mug.

'They're mad at me.' Emma raised her eyes to Dustin's.

'No, they're not, princess. They're processing, that's all. Most of the vampires in the bunker have heard about the Immortal families. They're taught to stay far away from them, because tussling with an Immortal is a sure way to get your head parted from your body.'

'I would never do that!'

'I know that, and they know that. They need time to think things through. They will realise you're not like the other Immortals. You're special.'

'I wish everyone would stop calling me that. I don't feel very special.'

Dustin's chuckle rumbled through his big chest. His wavy grey hair shifted around his face as he settled down onto the opposite end of the sofa and took a swig of his tea.

'Vampire lore is complex. The Codex talks about the Immortal families in such a way to drive terror through the beating heart of any man or the gaping hole of any vampire. They wrote it with that intent.'

'The Immortal families wrote the Vampire Codex?' Cara shifted in her seat with one eyebrow raised. 'I didn't know that.'

'Uh-huh. Any author worth their salt will frame their story to show their strengths and prowess. Every single one of the Immortal families created a section of the Codex. You've got the Hartfield family'—he waved his hand at Emma—'and the Astley, Deveroux, and Byron families. The Haven have also included their part in the history of vampires.'

Something tugged at Emma's subconscious as she listened to Dustin. The names of the Immortal families whirled through her mind until she latched on to the right memory.

'I recognise those names. After Flora was taken, I was searching through her stuff looking for clues, and I found an old journal. She had written a list of family names—those exact family names.'

'Does your grandmother know the truth about your lineage then?' Dustin asked.

'I don't know.' Emma took another sip of the hot tea. 'When I asked her why this was happening to me, she said she had her suspicions. She left me to get answers from her sources, but I'm not sure how much she knew.'

'Maybe she was stalling for time,' Cara suggested. 'Her daughter married an Immortal vampire and had a child. That's not the kind of secret you can keep from your family.'

'She was evasive after I got out of the hospital, but she knew what I'd become because she got me blood bags.' The memory of Flora telling her she was undead rattled around Emma's brain. Her grandmother had been so calm at the time, and it was only now that Emma had worked out that Flora must have known more than she was letting on. 'Let's say she was clued in on daddy dearest being a vampire. Why didn't she tell me? Why wait until I'd been bitten, murdered, and turned before looking for answers?'

'You told me you've always felt a darkness in your life. Perhaps Flora didn't have the heart to tell you that the fears you had were true and that darkness was your destiny.'

Emma pondered Cara's words. If Flora had been a loving and supportive grandparent, then Emma may have believed Flora had stayed silent to protect her. Flora hadn't been loving and supportive though. Flora had been simply going through the motions of a guardian, waiting for Emma to turn eighteen. So why keep quiet? Was it Flora's responsibility to kill Emma if she became an evil bloodsucker?

'I doubt it,' Emma mumbled. 'The only time she showed any interest in me was when she brought me home from the hospital with a rucksack full of blood!'

'Well, if Joey's information is correct, there's every chance she's safe and sound at Hartfield Manor. We need a plan to get her back,' Dustin said.

Dustin's voice was so calm that Emma almost believed it was possible, but from what Kai had said earlier, Hartfield Manor wasn't a place where you walked up to the front door and knocked.

'We'll work something out.' Cara lifted herself from the sofa and walked toward the rattling cage as it rose to meet them. 'First, we need to speak to James and get as much information out of Emma as we can.'

'I don't like the sound of that,' Emma said as she joined Cara by the bookshelf.

Dustin collected the empty cups and disappeared into his tiny kitchen. The noise of a running tap carried through the open door. Emma wanted to ask Dustin a bunch of questions about the Codex, her family, and what he thought of the entire situation, but the cage clunked into place and Cara strode inside. Emma knew she would have to wait for those answers.

'Catch up with you later, Dustin,' Cara shouted as she pulled the cage door closed.

The big man stuck his head around the door and smiled. 'Keep me updated on what James finds.'

The cage groaned and shifted before beginning its journey down to the Haven, giving Emma time to mull over the handsome vampire who was about to mess with her mind.

'How old is James?' she asked, trying to keep her voice neutral despite her interest being piqued.

'I'm not sure even he can remember.' Cara chuckled. 'He's older than Henric, though he doesn't look it.'

Emma recalled Henric's dated fashion sense—a consequence of being turned in the 1800s. James was stylish without being old-fashioned and appeared more connected to the current world than the other stuffy council leaders. Henric was old in every sense of the word, but James gave the ranks of the undead an altogether different vibe. If

James was older than Henric, then he had clearly surpassed the rules of transitioning.

'Will it hurt—whatever James does to me?'

Cara shook her head and leaned back against the cage wall.

'No, he'll lay his hands on your head and look into your mind. It's quick and painless. He'll be able to see repressed memories and pockets of your life your brain has locked away in the subconscious.'

'And you think I've got memories locked away inside my head?'

'Honestly? I don't know. Your father is an Immortal, and that must leave an imprint on your life in some way. Hopefully, James can find something that helps.'

The cage jolted to a halt as they arrived in the bunker. A bubbling sensation flooded through Emma's body as they strode toward the double doors. The now-familiar awareness of eyes watching her every movement washed over her, and she glanced at the mirrored glass, wondering which of the council leaders was watching them. Joey would have been able to tell her exactly who was behind the walls, but without his special gift, Emma was left guessing. Perhaps it was Henric observing the two of them returning after the rest of their group. Maybe it was the guard James had referred to. This could be how they monitored the main entrance.

It didn't matter who was watching them. The sensation slid beneath Emma's skin like a trickle of ice.

They walked on, passing the recreation hall and the living quarters before turning into a circular space with a bustling open-plan office stretching in all directions. This was the heart of the Haven's operations centre. Men and women sat at computer screens showing maps of the United Kingdom. Red circles pulsed in certain areas, and Emma thought they must indicate where the rogue half-bloods were.

The hum of overhead lights and computers merged with the soft chatter of conversation as the vampires on duty assessed the maps and went about their business.

Cara ignored them all and headed for a spiral staircase in the centre of the space. Looking up, Emma saw a mezzanine floor encased in glass. The windows here were also tinted, obscuring anyone who may be looking over the desks below.

They scaled the stairs and arrived on a small iron platform leading to a single door. As they approached, the door swung open to reveal a dimly lit room. James stood at the threshold. His long hair was tied back neatly as was his style. He wore dark jeans and a tight-fitting black shirt which accentuated his muscular torso.

'Ladies, what a lovely surprise.' James ushered them inside.

The ceiling was low where the room was cut out of the rock above them. Emma wondered if Dustin would even be able to fully stand up in here. A large mahogany desk stood to the right of the door. A leather chair spun slowly behind the desk, and Emma thought James must have vacated the chair before coming to greet them. Books and documents were spread across the entirety of the desk, and a brass lamp hunched over one faded yellow page.

To the left a curved sofa hugged the smooth line of the wall that overlooked a portion of the office space below. A glass table dominated the centre of the room with eight high-backed chairs. At her initial meeting with the Haven leaders, Emma had counted eight of them, including James. It reminded her of the tales of King Arthur and the Knights of the Round Table. Was this where the vampire leaders met to discuss their realm?

Tucked at the back of the room were a double bed and mahogany canopy. Deep red velvet curtains hung from the four wooden pillars, obscuring the satin sheets beyond. Emma felt suddenly uncomfortable like she had wandered into a boy's bedroom uninvited.

'What can I do for you?' James asked.

Turning toward the sound of his voice, Emma speculated if James may have an element of Simran's siren gift. His voice drew her in and held her attention like nobody else's. When he spoke, she listened.

'We've located the human,' Cara said. 'Unfortunately, it appears she is being held at Hartfield Manor.'

'I see.'

'It crossed my mind that Emma may have inaccessible memories that would help us extract the human from her current situation.'

'I see.' He glanced at Emma as she stood near the open door. 'And you want me to peek inside.'

'It might help.'

James held his hands together as if in prayer, pressing the tips of his middle fingers to his lips. He turned away from the girls and walked toward the tinted windows. Cara sent a quick look to Emma. Cara's jaw was tense, and her lips were drawn in a tight line. It was the first time Emma had seen Cara so unsure of herself.

The silence weighed Emma down until James eventually spoke again.

'I agree. You will leave Emma with me, and we will see what we can uncover together.'

Cara turned toward the door. Without looking back, she stepped onto the iron balcony and tugged the door shut behind her. Her boots clanged on every step as she rushed down the staircase and back across the office.

Emma was still staring at the closed door, almost willing it to open again, when her skin began to tingle. She knew James was watching her, but something stopped her from turning to look at him. It felt safe talking to him in the crowded recreation hall, but being here, alone in his living space, brought back memories of them in the hallway together. A simmering desire rose in Emma, but she wasn't ready to acknowledge it yet.

'You've got nothing to be afraid of Emma. I won't bite.'

She laughed and tried to relax.

'I'm not sure you'll be able to find anything in my head,' she lied, wringing her hands.

'There's no harm in trying.'

He extended a hand, inviting her to sit on the curved sofa. She perched on the edge and clasped her hands in her lap. When he lowered himself next to her, she shuffled on the spot, rearranging herself so her body was twisted to face him rather than being pressed against him.

The corners of his mouth twitched into a slight smile as he mirrored her actions, facing her and resting his elbow on the back of the sofa.

'What do you hope to discover from our session?'

Emma swallowed down the tremors that vibrated through her entire body.

'Cara thinks I may have information about my parents locked inside of me.'

'She's not wrong.' He leaned forward. 'Our birth is imprinted onto our brains, but because we are so young, it's a memory that is lost to all but a few.'

'You mean, you can recover what I saw the moment I was born?'

'Yes, that's exactly what I'm saying. We can take you back to the womb if you think it's necessary. Did your father ever sing or talk to your mother's belly when she was pregnant?'

Emma gaped at him. Was he serious? 'I have no idea. All Flora told me was my father died before I was born, and my mother died delivering me.'

'Okay, that's our starting point then.' He stood up and pulled two of the high-backed chairs away from the table. 'Sit here.'

Emma sat on one chair as James positioned the other directly opposite her, then sat. His knees extended down either side of her legs as he pulled the chair close. His breath brushed her face as he spoke, and it took all her concentration to stay focused. If he was digging about inside her mind, she didn't need him to see how affected she was by his close proximity.

'I need to place my hands on your head. Is that okay?'

Emma nodded, not trusting her voice.

'Close your eyes.'

She did as he instructed and tried to stop the churning thoughts that threatened to overwhelm her. What if he uncovered something terrible inside her mind? What if the darkness that had been such a massive part of her life was, in fact, pure evil and consumed anyone who encountered her?

Her mind went completely blank as James placed his cool hands on either side of her face.

He ran his fingers up toward her hairline, causing the tiny hairs on her neck to stand on end. Her stomach lurched alarmingly, and for a horrifying moment, she feared she might pass out.

Nothing registered. No smell, taste, nor audible sensation. It felt like she was in a bubble, just her and James. His fingers caressed her as he cupped them around the base of her skull. If she opened her eyes right now, she knew he would be close enough to kiss.

'Relax,' he said. 'I'm going to take you back now.'

She was floating or falling; she couldn't make up her mind which. Her body was weightless. She no longer felt the firm surface of the chair beneath her, nor the touch of her feet on the floor. The only thing anchoring her to the world was the sensation of James's fingers in her hair.

Her breathing was rough, coming in short, sharp gasps as if she had run a marathon and was nearing the finish line. When she thought it couldn't possibly be working, she found herself in a bright room. The harsh overhead lights flickered as a man in a mask and gown leaned over her. The creases around his eyes deepened as he smiled.

'*It's another girl,*' he said, looking at someone out of Emma's line of sight.

'*You have two beautiful baby girls.*'

'*Let me see,*' another voice said.

Flora's face floated into view, and Emma jerked back. James kept a firm grip on her head. She guessed it was so they wouldn't lose the connection.

'*She's beautiful,*' Flora said, scooping a baby into her arms. The view shifted, and Emma was looking down at her mother in the hospital bed. She was stunning. Her dark hair fanned out around her on the pillow. A sheen of sweat coated her face as she smiled. Dark circles ringed her eyes, but she looked happy, content.

'*Stop! You can't go in there.*' A loud voice echoed through the room as Flora spun toward the sound. A man stood in the delivery room doorway; he was tall with sandy blond hair that curled at the nape of his neck. A tattoo was just visible under the collar of his shirt. He wore a long, stained coat and held a blade that dripped blood onto the sterile floor.

'*You!*' Flora said.

'*No, please, you don't have to do this,*' Emma's mother pleaded.

Tears streamed down the man's face. His expression was a mix of regret and loathing. Emma's mother screamed as he lurched forward, plunging the knife into her heart. Blood oozed from her mouth as she twitched and bucked. Flora stumbled backwards into the doctor, who hustled them through a hospital curtain and into a long unlit corridor.

'*Run,*' he said. '*Keep Emma safe.*'

'*What about Amelia?*'

'*There's nothing we can do for her now.*'

The vision shifted once again, and Flora was running across a car park toward a car parked at the furthest streetlight. She bundled Emma into a baby seat and fired up the engine, driving away at great speed. Trees whistled by the windows as the car jostled her about.

Tears ran down Emma's face, but James maintained a firm grip on her head.

The visions came thick and fast, jumping from one day to the next. She saw Flora crying above her cot as she put her down to sleep and heard half of a conversation between her grandmother and a doctor called Bernie. She sensed the fear pulsating off Flora as she packed up their meagre belongings and left her home for a new one. The house that Emma had grown up in. The house Flora had told her had been their family home for generations. Lies. All of it. Her mother hadn't died in childbirth. She was murdered.

Emma let out a wracking sob and slumped forward into James's chest as he let go of her head. He wrapped his arms tightly around her body as she wept.

'I'm so sorry,' he whispered into her ear. 'I'm so, so sorry.'

• • •

The room was dark when Emma awoke, and it took her a few moments to get her bearings. The heavy velvet curtains cocooned her from the horrors of her life, and the black satin sheets felt cold against her skin. She was in James's bed—alone.

What the hell had she experienced? She had been a witness to her own birth, and an unwilling witness to the brutal death of her mother. Had that all really happened?

If it was true, then the web of lies Flora had told her about a dead father and a mother who'd lost her life in childbirth hurt more than she could put into words. Even the documents she had found in Flora's wrecked cabinet had confirmed the lie with a story of her mother's sacrifice.

'Are you okay?' James swept the curtain aside and sat on the edge of the bed.

Emma shook her head.

'Do you remember what you saw?'

'Yes,' she choked out.

'We were linked.' He took her hand and threaded his fingers into hers. 'I saw everything you saw.'

She blinked, and a fresh stream of hot tears trailed a path down her cheek. With his free hand, he rubbed his thumb under her eye to wipe away a tear, which made them fall even faster.

'She was murdered.'

'Yes,' James said, 'but Flora saved you.'

Something knotted deep inside Emma's chest, threatening to punch its way to the surface.

'My grandmother has always been so cold and cut off. I thought it was because she didn't want to be stuck with a kid.'

'Maybe the death of her daughter was too much to bear.'

Emma gasped and sat up straight, tightening her fingers around James's.

'Did you hear what the doctor said?' It was a redundant question; she saw it in his eyes.

'Two beautiful girls. I had a sister.'

7

The walk back to room seven felt like the final march down death row. Would Kai, Jess, Sim, and Dylan even let her through the door? Had Cara tried to smooth the tension with news of James and their quest to dig into her brain?

The new knowledge she had about her life left Emma with even more questions than she had before. It would no doubt be as much use as a wet paper bag in their mission to free Flora. She craved the support and camaraderie that she knew her friends were capable of. Had she lost their trust forever? All she could do was try to win it back, no matter what.

She heard the gentle murmur of conversation beyond the closed door as she stood in the corridor, readying herself to enter. Caring about people other than Flora was a new concept, and what they thought mattered more than she wanted to admit.

'Everything okay?' A soft voice pulled Emma from her musings, and she turned to find Katie standing before her.

'Yes, I'm fine, thank you,' she said with a tight smile. If the door opened and Jess saw her fraternising with the enemy, any hope of friendship would be over.

'You look a little lost.' Katie folded her arms across her chest.

It was a physical sign Emma knew well—a way to protect yourself in the subtlest of ways. Crossing your arms over where your heart would, or should, be was a clear indication of anxiety and a desire to protect yourself from harm.

Emma stepped away from the door and gave Katie her full attention, making the small girl move back in surprise.

'Are *you* okay?' Something was nagging at Emma, and it had played on her mind since seeing the young vampire in the lecture hall.

Katie hugged her arms tighter around her body and scanned the corridor. 'Me? I'm fine. Why do you ask?'

'You seem nervous.' Emma wondered if that was even possible for a member of the undead. 'Were you looking for Jess?'

Katie ran her hands up and down her arms as if trying to add warmth to her bones like a human would. 'No, why would I—' She dropped her gaze. 'Is she okay? I didn't mean to hurt her.'

Without knowing the details of Jess's love life, it was going to be difficult for Emma not to dig a deep hole for herself in this conversation, but she suspected Katie had wanted to talk about Jess.

'Oh, you know Jess.' Emma hoped she sounded like the kind of friend Jess would have confided in. 'She's a survivor. Nothing keeps her down for long.' Even though she couldn't be sure if Jess's romantic dealings were as ruthless as her other skills, she truly believed what she'd said.

'That's good to hear. When Pierce banned me from seeing her, I—' Katie's eyes grew wide as she realised her error.

'Why did Pierce ban you from being together?'

'He didn't! Oh no…please, you can't tell her. I'll get in trouble, and I can't afford to be banished from the Haven.'

'Banished? They wouldn't kick you out of here for falling in love with another vampire.'

'Of course not, but they would kick me out for falling in love with one of Cara's vampires.'

'What do you mean?'

'I've said too much.' Katie took a step back.

Emma grabbed her by the arm, threw open the door to number seven, and pushed the small vampire inside.

'What the hell?' Dylan jumped up from the sofa.

'Katie!' Jess gasped, stiffening her posture as Katie stumbled to a halt in the middle of the living room.

Katie hugged her arms so tightly around herself that Emma feared she would break her own ribs. Dylan and Kai blocked the door, and Simran was on her feet and in Emma's face before she had time to blink.

'What's going on?' Simran hissed, her eyes flicking between Katie and Jess.

'Tell them,' Emma said. 'Tell them how Pierce forbid you from seeing Jess.'

'Is this true?' Jess turned on her ex-girlfriend.

Katie backed herself into a corner before sliding down the wall. She cradled her knees to her chest, and for the first time, Emma wondered how young the girl had been when she was turned.

'It's true. By order of the council. The entire bunker has been warned off Cara's nest. Nobody is allowed to get too close to any of you until further notice.' She buried her face into her knees and sobbed.

Everyone remained still. Jess broke the spell by rushing to Katie's side and pulling the girl into a tight hug. Her soft sobs filled the silence.

Cara appeared in the doorway of her bedroom with a deep frown etched on her beautiful face.

'They're cutting us off,' Cara said. 'I've only ever seen this happen once before, many years ago. A team was assigned to hunt down—'

'Hunt down what?' Kai asked.

'An Immortal,' Cara answered, looking directly at Emma. 'It appears the Haven council thinks our time is limited because of our mission.'

'Bullshit!' Dylan stormed across the room, threading his fingers through his hair as he paced back and forth. 'They're expecting us to fail without giving us a chance.'

'We're going up against an Immortal family, of course we're going to fail!' Simran mumbled.

'No, we're not,' Emma said. Her voice was strong and steady despite the whirling sensations that threatened to unravel her. 'This particular Immortal family has one weakness that we can use against them.'

'And what's that?' Dylan asked. Scepticism dripped from his voice.

'Me!'

Everyone stared at Emma as she lifted her chin. It was as if all the pieces of her life had fallen into place. It was oddly satisfying to be a major part of the puzzle, and possibly a pivotal piece that might be used as a weapon.

'Joey said Flora was still alive. They must need her to get to me. I'm the bait. Use me to get inside Hartfield Manor.'

'I'm not risking your life on a foolish task,' Cara strode across the floor to pick up a sheaf of paper from the coffee table. 'Anyway, the fact that you have been a vampire for only a matter of days makes you the least qualified to be bait. Having said that—'

'You're not actually considering it, are you?' Kai studied Cara as she scanned the pages. 'You are, aren't you?'

'Not at all!' Cara cracked her neck from side to side. 'Okay, maybe I am.'

'You can't be serious,' Kai said. 'You'd be sending Emma into danger. She's not prepared or trained for that kind of mission.'

'Don't you think I know that?' Cara's jaw was tight as she spoke. 'We're running out of options. Henric wants the old lady, but judging by his order'—she waved her hand in Katie's direction—'he doesn't think we'll succeed.'

'Why is Henric so keen to speak to my grandmother?' Emma asked. It wasn't until that moment she fully grasped that their mission revolved around the safety of one human. It was something that no vampire should care about, but the Haven had assigned their elite team to this mission. What did Flora know that was so important to the Haven?

'I don't know. Involving humans in vampire business is unprecedented. Apart from the Revenants, the Haven has no dealings with humankind,' Cara said.

'Dustin might know,' Emma said, remembering the one human link they still had. 'There might be something in the Codex about it.'

Cara appeared to mull this over as she looked around her assembled team. 'You're right. We need more intel before we send Emma into the lion's den. Kai, Emma, you two speak to Dustin. Jess, you need to return Katie to her nest. Be discreet. Dylan and I will get in touch with our sources in the field and see if anyone has heard anything.'

'What do you need me to do?' Simran tossed her dark hair over her shoulder.

Everyone glanced at Cara as she smiled at Sim with a devious glint in her eye. 'I need you to have a little conversation with Henric,' she said.

'Gladly. He'll spill all his juicy secrets before I'm done with him.'

'Use caution, Sim. If anyone sees what you're doing, you'll be punished. There's nothing I can do to prevent it,' Cara said.

'Got it. I'll be careful.' Simran spun on her heels and disappeared through the front door.

Cara's voice boomed across the living space. 'You have your orders. What are you waiting for?'

• • •

The cage jolted to a halt, and Kai pulled back the door. Dustin was waiting with his usual warm welcome.

'Back so soon.' He chuckled. 'It's the tea, isn't it?'

Emma giggled and followed him into the small living room. There was no fire in the hearth today, and the curtains at the cottage windows were drawn back to reveal a beautiful sunny day. *Daytime.* It struck Emma that she no longer recognised if it was day or night. Living in the bunker meant no windows to the outside world. They fed when they were hungry, but in truth, Emma had no idea if it was breakfast, lunch, or dinnertime. Perhaps the feral vampires on the moors were better off.

'What can I do for you both?'

'Cara sent us,' Kai said. 'We need information, and we think you might be able to help us get it.'

Kai took a seat in one of the armchairs. His black hair and pale face stood out in contrast to the floral fabric.

'Okay, shoot. What do you want to know?'

'Why is the Haven so interested in Emma's grandmother?'

Dustin scratched his beard. His big frame towered over the pair as he stood in the centre of the room and looked down at them.

'Okay then.' Dustin pulled a pair of steel-rimmed glasses out of his breast pocket and pushed them up the bridge of his nose. 'Let's see what we can find.'

Emma was expecting him to pull out a stack of old books with worn leather bindings, so when Dustin grabbed a laptop from his bag, she was disappointed.

'Are you googling the answers?' A smile tugged at the corner of Emma's mouth.

'You may be a princess, but being cheeky won't get you the answers any faster.' Dustin chuckled as his fingers flew across the keys. 'I'm logged in to the Haven mainframe, so if there are any files, updates, or messages referring to your grandmother, we'll see them.'

Emma and Kai watched him work. The screen shifted and changed as he pored over document after document. It was mesmerising to watch.

'Cara told us about your meeting with James,' Kai whispered, breaking into the silence as Dustin continued his task. 'How did it go?'

'It was terrifying and fascinating all at once. James worked his mojo on me and managed to take me back to when I was born. It turns out my mother was murdered in her hospital bed, and Flora snatched me away to safety.'

Kai's face mirrored her own feelings of shock. She had been trying to process what she had learned, but it was unfathomable. Who would want to murder her mother?

'I'm so sorry. It must be unnerving to find out everything you thought you knew about your life was wrong.'

Emma was relieved that someone seemed to understand how she felt. Unnerved was the right word. All her life she had believed what Flora had spoon-fed her, but none of it was true.

'The vision showed me more.' Emma was determined to no longer hide anything from her friends. 'When my grandmother took me, she was concerned about the other baby she left behind…my twin sister.'

'Whoa, that's deep.'

'Yeah, it was hard enough watching some evil monster butcher my mother, but finding out at the same time that I had a sister is taking a while to sink in.'

'What happened to her?'

'I don't know. I came out of the vision. I guess she was killed along with my mother. It was all pretty brutal. I doubt anyone made it out of that room alive.'

'Apart from you and Flora,' Kai said.

'You might be onto something there, Kai,' Dustin said.

'What do you mean?' Kai sat forward in the chair.

'I've come across correspondence dated nearly eighteen years ago between the Haven and a secure email address talking about an assassination attempt. I can't find out who the recipient was, but I'd bet a packet of custard creams that they're talking about you and your mother.'

'I was meant to die, but Flora saved me.'

'They're covering something up, but I don't know what,' Dustin said.

'So, when I was attacked in the alley and killed by that psycho vamp, it was this assassination attempt catching up with me?' Emma's head started to spin.

'Maybe.' Dustin took his glasses off and polished them on the corner of his shirt. 'But that doesn't explain why another vampire turned you.'

He went back to the laptop and clicked on a few zip folders, muttering under his breath as he opened and closed each one in turn.

'Aha!' Dustin stabbed a meaty finger at the screen. 'We have a winner!'

Kai and Emma peered at the screen as a document loaded with the subject heading *[Hartfield: Test Subject]*.

'It looks like you were some sort of an experiment, princess,' Dustin said.

'Gross. What kind of experiment?' A sliver of ice travelled down her spine as she waited for Dustin to peruse the document. Was this why she had always felt the darkness around her? Had she been created in some weird test tube and destined to wreak havoc on the world?

'Oh.' Dustin leaned back in his chair, scratching his beard again. It was a sign Emma was starting to see as uncertainty. 'It looks like the Hartfields had been trying to breed with humans for centuries, but the babies and mothers always died. For some reason, your mother's genes were compatible, and she survived the pregnancy and delivery.'

The room was silent as Emma processed Dustin's words.

'Are you saying my mother was murdered because she didn't die in delivery?'

'It certainly points to that,' Dustin said quietly. 'From what it says on the document, all the Immortal families have tried to create a Dhampir. Nobody had ever succeeded—until you were born.'

Emma stood and paced the floor. Beads of sweat gathered on her brow and snaked their way down the sides of her forehead. A wave of intense, raw anger clawed at her chest, making her skin feel like it was about to catch fire.

'There's a photograph attachment,' Dustin said, scrolling further down the screen.

As the image loaded, Emma swallowed down the churning horror that crowded the corners of her brain.

The picture filled the screen, and Emma froze. Flora had shown her photographs of her mother, but she had always told her that her father had hated having his picture taken. To see her parents together for the first time took Emma's breath away. The man was tall, well-built with sandy blond hair that flicked out at the nape of his neck. The photograph was taken in the summer sunshine. Her mother wore a pretty sundress, and the man wore only jeans, leaving his chest bare. Covering his right arm and winding up his neck was a tattoo—a swirling mass of thorn branches and wilting blooms.

'I've seen this man before,' Emma said.

'According to this file, he's your father.'

'He can't be.' Panic rose in her voice. 'I remember him from my vision. He's the man who murdered my mother.'

• • •

In the world of humans, the sun shone, the birds sang, and holidaymakers trampled the grounds of Whitby Abbey. But in the world of vampires, the Haven residents slept, renewing their energy for their next mission at sunset.

Behind the door of number seven, however, six vampires remained wide awake.

'I can't believe coffee actually suppresses blood cravings,' Emma muttered as she drained her fourth cup of the day.

'It's no substitute for the real thing, so make sure you mix it up.' Dylan tossed her a blood bag from the fridge.

'Tell me again what Henric said.' Cara positioned Simran in a prime spot on the sofa and gave the girl her full attention.

'I faked a tiny attack of doubt and insecurity about my nest's mission, and he lapped it up.' Simran smiled slyly. 'He thinks we're doomed, and this mission to rescue Flora from the Hartfields' clutches will be the death of us all.'

'Well, that's reassuring to hear from our great and wise leader!' Kai slumped onto the sofa next to Simran and lay his head back to stare up at the ceiling. 'Why give us this mission if they thought we wouldn't survive it?'

'Honestly? He hopes Emma will get herself killed, and the Immortal family will be happy with that and leave the rest of us alone. Sorry, Em,' Simran said.

Emma shrugged and drained her cup. 'He's right. I'm an untrained one-month-old vampire. I'm amazed I haven't died already!'

Cara rolled her eyes before urging Simran to continue.

'He said the council is divided over Emma. Most of them want her gone because they think the Hartfields will find out she's here and attack, but there is a small faction who want to protect Emma.'

'James,' Emma muttered.

'Yes. It seems James has developed a soft spot for our newbie roommate, and nobody, not even Henric, will go against him,' Simran said.

'Jeez, what did the two of you do during this mind-meld of yours?' Dylan winked.

'Funny. I'll have you know he was a perfect gentleman and very supportive after I witnessed my father *murder* my mother,' said Emma.

Dylan's sheepish smile softened Emma's escalating rage, and she gave him a playful nudge as she sat on the chair beside him.

'The mind-meld taught me two things,' Emma continued. 'My dad killed my mum, and Flora has been shielding me from the truth. I'm not sure how that helps our current situation or why that marks me as someone who must be assassinated.'

'Maybe the tests weren't meant to be successful, and the Immortal families are getting rid of the evidence,' suggested Jess. 'If nobody other than your mum survived the pregnancy and childbirth, then it could be a simple cleanup mission.'

'Dustin said *all* the Immortal families have tried at some point to create a Dhampir,' Kai added. 'Why get rid of something when you're the first one in the race to win the prize?'

Emma dropped her cup, spilling the dregs of coffee across the floor.

'They weren't trying to get rid of me.' Emma's mind flicked through the possibilities. 'Yes, I was killed, but my attacker was interrupted. Someone else killed him, and then fed me their blood.'

'Of course.' Dylan slapped his hand on the breakfast bar as his thoughts caught up with Emma's. 'You were still human—no good to an Immortal family. They didn't want to assassinate you—'

'They wanted to turn you,' Cara finished.

'You told me yourself that my vampire lineage was inside me but remained dormant,' Emma's voice rose as the pieces began to slide into place. 'They needed to wake me up and release the Dhampir.'

'But why?' Jess asked.

'I guess we better find out,' Cara said. 'I think you need to speak to James again, Emma. If he's truly looking out for you, then open up to him about our findings and see if he can unlock anything else useful to us. We need confirmation that your theory is right, and a Dhampir can be awoken. Otherwise, we're back to square one and you're still at the top of the assassination list.'

Before Emma could answer, the shrill sound of an alarm tore through the air. The lights flickered on and off before bathing the room in a deep red that resembled blood.

'What the hell is that?' Emma asked.

Cara was on her feet in seconds. She ripped open the cupboard doors on the sideboard and pulled out a selection of wooden stakes and swords.

'That's the cottage alarm. Someone has breached the exterior,' she yelled, handing out the weapons.

'Dustin!' Emma cried.

'He's trained for this,' Dylan said above the din. 'He'll be okay.'

Emma gripped the hilt of a sword and studied her reflection in the blade. She looked strong and fierce on the outside, a small rim of red glowing in her eyes, but on the inside, she was terrified. What if whoever wanted her had killed Dustin? She didn't think she would recover from that.

Kai opened the front door, and the friends poured out into the corridor. Vampires were running in every direction. Trepidation and fear hung thick in the air as everyone tried to find their place in the panic. At the far end of the corridor, Emma spotted Katie and her nest running toward the recreation hall. Her petite frame was swallowed up in the chaos.

'This way,' Cara shouted, pushing against the flow of the crowd swarming after Pierce like he was the Pied Piper.

'The cage is the other way,' Emma yelled back.

'We can't compromise the main door. Dustin would never reveal that entrance. To get topside, we need to use the stairs and tunnels,' said Cara.

They pushed through a plain wooden door Emma hadn't noticed before and rushed along the dark corridor beyond. The space was cold and damp, cut out of the ground and left as raw as the day it was made. Every fifty yards there was a sputtering lamp connected to loose wires that trailed along the top of the wall. It was evident these tunnels were rarely used.

When they arrived at a stone staircase buried into the wall, Cara hissed, 'Up! Dylan, you go first. Check it out, but be careful.'

Dylan vanished up the stairs, and the rest of the group followed. Even without Dylan's superpower, they still made good progress. The sound of the alarm grew fainter the higher they climbed.

At the top of the stairs, they were greeted by a hatch. It was closed, which meant Dylan must have closed it behind him. Cara lifted the lid a fraction, keeping her head low as she glanced around the area beyond the stairs.

'Clear!' She thrust open the hatch door, and the stairwell flooded with daylight. Whoever had set the alarms off had attacked during the day knowing the vampires would be asleep underground.

Emma stumbled out into a wooded area. The exterior of Dustin's cottage rose in the distance, with the imposing structure of Whitby Abbey on the horizon. People milled around the ruins and walked along the clifftop paths. It was the perfect cover for an attacker making their escape.

'Whoever attacked is long gone,' Dylan said as he reappeared at their side, 'but Dustin is pretty badly injured.'

The group darted from the cover of the trees and burst through the cottage door. The cosy interior Emma had grown to love was in disarray. Chair legs littered the floor as if someone had used the furniture as a weapon. The charred logs from the fireplace were scattered across the floor, disturbing the cat bed. The cat was nowhere to be seen.

Dustin's sofa now balanced precariously on its side against the far wall, as if it had been picked up and thrown across the room. Thankfully, it's current placement meant the hidden entrance to the elevator was blocked.

A groan drifted across the broken pieces of the room, and the group of friends turned toward the small kitchen area.

Dustin lay on the floor, his face a bruised and bloody mess. His right eye was swollen shut, and he had clearly taken quite a beating on his right side. Fresh blood poured from a gash in his hairline. His grey hair was now stained a deep red.

'Who did this?' Cara asked as she gently tended to Dustin's wounds.

'Hooded.' Dustin's voice cracked with the strain of talking. 'Couldn't see.'

Emma felt the familiar sensation of ice flood through her veins at the mention of a hooded assailant. Was the mysterious hooded stranger who turned her into a vampire the same one who had left this carnage and hurt her friend?

The cottage door slammed open behind them, and the group drew their weapons in readiness. Pierce and his nest stood in the doorway, assessing the room. Their faces reflected the devastation Emma had felt when she'd entered the cottage moments before.

Everyone relaxed and lowered their weapons.

'We've secured the perimeter.' Pierce spoke to Cara, team leader to team leader. 'No one breached the bunker.'

'Thank you, Pierce. Would you be able to call for an ambulance? Dustin needs more help than I can offer him.'

He nodded and pulled a phone from his pocket, stepping outside as he hit the numbers. Katie and Jess locked eyes as the rest of the team left the small confines of the living room, and Emma pondered Henric's orders to not get close to Cara's team. Was this the start of it? Would the bad guys—her family—take them out one by one?

Kai and Jess busied themselves with wrapping Dustin's wounds the best they could with the meagre contents of his first aid box. Dylan and Emma began putting the furniture back in place and clearing up the debris. If the police arrived with the ambulance, it needed to look like a human robbery and attack rather than a supernatural invasion.

Emma placed a bag of broken crockery outside the front door and took a moment to enjoy the sun on her face and the sound of the sea crashing on the rocks below the abbey.

Even though her head was starting to thump from being outside, she knew she had fed enough before the alarm had gone off. When the paramedics arrived, she wouldn't be whisked away in the back of the ambulance with blood pouring from her eyes. Standing in the sunshine was a simple act that filled her cold, dead heart with joy. Emma relished the warmth, closing her eyes and raising her face to the sky.

The itch beneath her skin started at her fingertips and trailed its way up her arms. Someone was watching her. Over the last couple of days, Emma had been testing her powers to see if there were any subtle differences in how her superpower felt. She had ascertained that when one of her friends watched her, the feeling was neutral like the warmth of the sun on her skin, or a soft caress. If it was an unknown person or volatile threat, her body reacted uniquely. Her nerve endings would vibrate, the fine hairs on her skin would rise, and a chill would run down her spine giving her a warning response. Right now, her body was giving her a warning as loud as the alarm in the bunker.

She moved slightly to her left and glanced inside the cottage to see how close her friends were. Simran was in the doorway sweeping up a broken vase. Jess and Kai were still in the kitchen with Dustin, and Cara was hovering with Dylan at the back of the room near the bookcase and the hidden elevator.

'I feel something,' Emma said as quietly as possible but loud enough that Simran would hear. 'Someone is watching us.'

Simran lifted her head at Emma's words and set the broom aside. She grabbed a wooden stake and slid it into her belt. She nodded at Emma before walking to the open door.

They stood side by side acting as natural as possible; two friends standing on the doorstep admiring the view.

'Which way?' Simran asked.

'They're inside the abbey ruins.'

'The place is crawling with humans. Are you sure it isn't a tourist?'

'No, it feels different. Cold and sinister.'

Simran glanced at her but said nothing. A blur of movement caused them both to stand to attention.

'There. Left of the furthest column... Oh my God!'

'What? What do you see?'

'It's Flora!'

Emma set off running before Simran could stop her. She heard Simran calling for Cara and the shouts of her friends as they stumbled out of the cottage in pursuit.

She ran, keeping her speed to a fast human pace so as not to freak out the dog walkers and history buffs who swarmed the area.

Jumping over the uneven ground and fallen masonry, Emma slowed as she approached her grandmother. Flora's face was bruised. Her lips were stretched thin, and her brow was pulled taut as she glared at Emma as if in warning. She had acted on instinct rather than assessing the situation. Cara would rip her a new one for acting so foolishly and putting them all in danger. Perhaps Henric was right, and today was the day Emma Hartfield died.

'Are you really here?' Emma spoke so quietly that there was no way Flora could have heard her, but it was strange to see her grandmother again after everything that had happened.

'She's here.' A new voice filled the air behind Emma, and she spun to face the threat.

The world crashed to a halt as she stared at the girl standing before her. It wasn't possible; she had to be dreaming or hallucinating at least. Emma was looking into her own face. The hair was different, short and choppy. The clothes were almost utilitarian in style, but there was no denying who the girl standing in front of Emma was. It was like looking in a mirror. This was her twin sister—the one she and James assumed had died with their mother in the hospital.

'Finally, we meet.' She spoke in a quiet voice, almost hypnotic in its hushed tone. It was a whisper that made you want to lean in despite the cold, hard edge to it. Something Emma was sure many humans had fallen for at their peril.

'Amelia?'

The girl smiled, but instead of it being a natural action, it looked alien on her face, like her lips had never performed the act before.

'What do you want?' Emma moved her hand to the wooden stake secured in her back pocket. Although she knew who this girl was, she was also a stranger—a danger to everyone.

The girl was fast, too quick for Emma. In one fluid movement, Amelia manoeuvred around her and disarmed Emma, flinging the stake out of reach. In another step, she was at Flora's side. The old lady flinched violently as Amelia wrenched Flora's arm behind her back.

Dylan was first to arrive at Emma's side. His face was a mask of disbelief at what he was seeing. Cara, Simran, and Kai arrived a few moments later.

Emma held her hands out in front of her in an act of submission, keeping her eyes locked on the girl's face despite the rising thundering beat of Flora's heart.

'You're my sister.' Emma took a tentative step forward.

The girl snarled and pulled on Flora's arm until the old lady screamed.

'Please, please don't hurt her. She's *our* grandmother.'

Amelia laughed and shoved Flora to the floor, standing over her as a vulture hovers over its dinner. She gripped the collar of her coat and pulled a dark hood over her head.

'It was you!' Emma gasped, recognising her as the mysterious hooded stranger who had turned her into a vampire. 'Why?' Emma struggled against the sting of tears and the burn at the back of her throat. 'Why did you do this to me?'

'That's what family are for,' Amelia said. 'I wasn't about to let my dear sister die. The party has only just begun, and this is merely the appetiser.'

In a blur she disappeared, lost in the ruins of the abbey. She blended into her surroundings like a ghost, her words lingering in the air.

8

Flora had been in the meeting with Henric and the council leaders for hours. Emma paced back and forth outside the room until she made herself dizzy.

'You need to calm down.' Cara's voice was firm and grounded. 'They have a lot of questions for your grandmother.'

'Like what? What could she possibly know about a world that belongs to vampires?' It was a question that had driven Emma to distraction as they had cleaned up Flora's cuts and brought her down in the cage to meet with Henric.

'Her daughter—your mother—married an Immortal. She *must* know something! Because the Immortal families are all about destroying half-bloods, Henric will be eager to find out what she knows.'

Emma sat on one of the chairs outside the meeting room doors and crossed her arms over her chest. Nothing made sense to her anymore. A few weeks ago, all she'd had to worry about was which university she would attend. Now, she was a vampire living in a hidden underground bunker. She had an evil twin, and her grandmother had knowledge of a secret and dangerous supernatural world.

'Have you heard any news about Dustin?' Emma tried to distract herself from the uncertainty.

'He's doing great.' Cara smiled. 'Should be home in the morning.'

'He'll be happy about that.' Emma chuckled, remembering how it took three of them to get him in the back of the ambulance.

Dustin had argued about going with the paramedics, trying to brush off his wounds as mere scratches. He'd overlooked the simple fact that he had needed twenty stitches in his head, had broken four ribs, and had only one eye open.

The door handle turned. Emma and Cara shot to their feet before James had time to step over the threshold.

'Emma, I wonder if I might have a quick word.' He closed the door behind him. Emma got a brief glimpse of her grandmother sitting in the same seat Emma had occupied not that long ago.

'Sure, what is it?'

With one look from James, Cara excused herself, leaving them alone in the waiting room. Emma's nerves began to tingle beneath her skin.

'Flora is doing great.' He smiled genuinely. 'She's tough for a human.'

Emma nodded but said nothing. Her senses were on full alert as she tried to read James's expression.

'There have been a few revelations here today. Information that will cause you some distress, yet I think you're more than capable of handling it.'

Emma wondered if the rest of the Haven council expected her to be freaked out by whatever Flora was sharing in there. It unsettled her. Had James been given the role of being her knight in shining armour?

It was nice to know one of the oldest vampires in the bunker had her back, but she also wanted to prove that she was strong, fierce, and capable in these testing times.

Standing face-to-face with her twin sister had been an enormous shock. Through her mind-meld with James, she had believed Amelia had perished with their mother. Did James feel responsible for pulling those memories from her mind? Is that what he meant by distressing revelations?

'It's come to light'—he took a step closer to her—'that Flora was a dear friend of Charlotte Hartfield, your mother, but wasn't related to her.'

He observed Emma as she processed his words. The impact of every syllable hit her in the gut until she dropped to her knees with a loud sob.

'I'm sorry.' James knelt beside her on the ground.

Emma hadn't had much in her life, but she had always had Flora—a woman who didn't have a maternal bone in her body. She had left Emma to raise herself with minimal input or guidance, but she had always been around, like a comforting blanket made of flesh and bone.

She wasn't sure how much more she could take. Finding Flora had been the only thing holding her together. The family bond that had been so important to Emma was slipping through her fingers, and everything she had been led to believe was a lie.

Dead father was an Immortal vampire.

Dead mother had been murdered by her father.

Dead twin sister had been alive all this time.

No grandmother. No family. *No one.*

'Please, can you take me away from here?' Emma wiped the tears from her eyes. 'I need to get far away from the Haven, from Flora, from vampires.'

James offered her his hand.

• • •

The view was spectacular. Emma gazed out across the black ocean that stretched for miles. It had felt good to climb up to the whalebone arch; the burn in her legs felt like a normal human reaction.

They found a bench and sat in companionable silence. Emma was relieved that the streets had been clear on their walk through the harbour. No traffic, no people, just James. He was the silent rock who calmed her down by merely providing his company.

'I'm sorry.' She looked down at the twinkling lights in the bay.

'Why are you apologising?'

'I'm sure there are a million things you need to be doing back at the Haven instead of babysitting an emotional teen vamp with family issues.'

James chuckled in that intensely velvety way Emma loved so much.

'There isn't a vampire in that bunker who doesn't have issues of one kind or another. Just because you're struggling with what's happening to you at the moment doesn't make it any less important.'

'Thanks. I guess I'm not used to having anyone around who's got my back. If I ever had a problem, I had to work through it on my own.'

'You're not alone anymore, Emma.'

She glanced at him. His face was partially covered by shadows from the clouds drifting across the moon. He was handsome and mysterious, not in a good-looking Paul Parker way, but deeper. An old soul wrapped in a young body, preserved against the harshness of life.

He turned and caught her staring at him, but Emma didn't look away. His gaze flicked across her face, settling on her lips, and before she had time to speak, he leaned in and kissed her. She was rooted to the spot. A million thoughts crowded her already overpopulated brain.

The kiss was soft and gentle with a tenderness to it that surprised Emma. As James began to pull away, she knew she wasn't ready for this moment to be over. She kissed him back, testing the waters with another gentle caress to see if he realised what he had done and regretted it. He responded with a light moan that shot along Emma's spine, igniting every cell in her body. His hands moved to her face. One cupped her cheek and the other wound into her hair at the nape of her neck. The kiss became deeper, stronger, harder.

They sat on the hilltop entwined in each other's arms, entranced in this moment and lost in each other. Nothing else existed. No vampires. No Haven. No Flora. There was only James, kissing her with a passion and desire she had only ever read about in books.

When they did come up for air, Emma's head spun. The gaping hole in her chest where her heart no longer beat ached with a sensation that was alien to her, yet not unpleasant.

James's hair had fallen loose and hung around his shoulders, framing his face. He looked like a young boy, and Emma's throat tightened. She had never felt like this before. She didn't know she *could* feel like this. Pesky emotions only got in the way—wasn't that what she had believed all these years?

'I'm sorry. I shouldn't have done that,' he said, slightly breathless.

'Now it's you who shouldn't be apologising.'

He smiled at her as he tucked a strand of hair behind her ear. 'You've got enough going on without me confusing things for you.'

'This isn't confusing.' She waved her hand between them. 'Everything back at the Haven and Hartfield Manor—that's the confusing part. Sitting here with you, I feel more in control, like everything is okay.'

He slipped his arm around her shoulder and pulled her close. They sat side by side, looking out at the horizon. She nestled her head on his shoulder and breathed in his scent.

'Flora might not be your biological grandmother, but she did take you from the hospital that day and kept you safe all these years.'

Emma knew he spoke the truth. She had even had the same thought, but the deception still cut deep.

'I know,' she whispered. 'She only ever had my best interests at heart, and I've already forgiven her for not telling me the truth. It still hurts. Betrayal is the worst way to hurt the ones you love.'

'Sometimes people don't mean to betray you. Sometimes they believe they're doing something for the right reasons, even if they do end up causing harm.'

Emma sat up and faced James, staring into those eyes that seemed to see her as nobody else could.

'What's going to happen to Flora?' She hadn't thought about it until that moment. Now that her fictional grandmother was safe, did Henric and the Haven still need her? Did they consider a human with knowledge of their world a threat? Yes, Emma was hurt, angry, and upset with Flora, but she still loved the woman.

'I'll deal with it. I'll recommend that Flora is taken back home to Allendale, or if she wants to relocate for her own safety, then I can arrange that. The Haven has no further use for her.'

Part of her felt an enormous sense of relief, but another part of her, the old human part, realised with a start that she would not be going back with Flora. Their journey together had come to an abrupt end. Seventeen years and now it was over. There would be no more Allendale. No more Flora with her quirky ways, artist smocks, and incense sticks. Emma belonged to the Haven now.

'What happens to me?'

James cupped her face in his hands and kissed her tenderly on the lips. 'I'll keep you safe. Should anyone from Hartfield Manor want you, they'll have to come through me first.'

He kissed her again, and she melted into him. The bench, Whitby Abbey, and their surroundings melted into nothing as she gave her heart over completely. If this was love, then she never wanted it to end.

All her life she had pushed against the world, never letting anyone in. The darkness that swirled through her, the same darkness that she had feared for so long, now consumed her in a different way. There would be no more fear, no more mistrust, no more shutting everyone out. Was it possible that she had finally found her place in the world?

• • •

Emma walked down the corridor toward room seven, wondering if her friends would notice the change in her. She and James had been gone for hours. Her hair was tousled, her lips were swollen from kissing him, and if she were still human, her face would be flushed.

Despite the horrors that had unfolded over the last few hours—Dustin's attack, Amelia's appearance, Flora's revelation—Emma had never felt more alive.

She had no idea if her relationship, if you could call it that, with James would cause conflict in Cara's nest, so she decided to keep it to herself for the time being. There was enough to deal with without adding her love life into the mix.

The door opened as she reached for the handle, and Dylan stood in the doorway with a big cheesy grin across his face.

'She's back,' he shouted over his shoulder before winking at Emma.

Was she that obvious? Were their vampire powers so strong that they revealed when someone had been intimate with another?

'We thought you'd done a runner on us and taken James with you.' Dylan chuckled. 'Sim reckoned you'd kidnapped him in exchange for your old life.'

Simran flicked her hair over her shoulder and shrugged. 'I said that's what I would do, not what I thought Em would do.'

'No kidnapping.' Emma smiled. 'James is safely back in the Haven and meeting with Henric as we speak.'

She took a deep breath. She waited for one of them to notice how her voice had changed when she'd mentioned his name, or how she'd shuffled her feet and wrung her hands when she had talked about him. Either they didn't notice, or they had chosen to ignore it. Emma was glad that everything appeared normal.

'We were sorry to hear about Flora.' Jess stepped forward to pull Emma into a tight embrace. 'I know how hurt I was when Katie lied, so finding out Flora isn't your real grandmother must suck.'

'Thanks.' Emma was grateful they understood. 'It's the strangest feeling though. I'm not mad anymore. That news should have crushed me, and in my previous life it would have, but coming here and meeting you guys… I guess it's softened the blow.'

'We've said it all along, Em.' Dylan tugged her out of Jess's hug and slid his arm around her in his usual friendly manner. 'We're your family now, and you can always count on us.'

A warmth settled in Emma's chest as she studied the faces in the room. Dylan's warm eyes sparkled as he squeezed her to him. Jess and Simran, the yin and yang of their group, smiled at her with such tenderness and genuine affection that it took Emma's breath away. Family. That's all she had ever wanted—a real family. One that couldn't be harmed or corrupted by the darkness she felt in her soul.

'I wouldn't have survived this long as a vampire if it hadn't been for you guys,' Emma said. 'Thank you.'

The girls rushed forward to join the group hug, and they were all still laughing when Kai and Cara burst through the door.

'The PDA will have to wait until later,' Cara said with a serious note to her voice. 'We've got a mission.'

The energy in the room changed, and everyone snapped into work mode. If Cara had a mission, then it was pertinent to Emma's situation.

'I received a message from Joey,' Cara said. 'He says he must speak to us about something going on at Hartfield Manor. It appears that our chat with him on the moors the other night encouraged him to do some investigating of his own.'

'What did he find?' Jess asked.

'He said the manor is becoming more active.'

'Active? What the hell does that mean?' Dylan sat on the sofa and spread a large roll of paper out across the coffee table—blueprints of Hartfield Manor.

They surrounded the table and reviewed the images.

'Joey thinks they're taking half-bloods to this compound on the grounds.' Cara pointed to a set of outbuildings at the back of the main house.

'I thought Immortals were at war with half-bloods, so why capture them instead of killing them straight away?' Emma asked.

'The only goal the Immortal families have is to rid the world of half-blood vampires. I don't know why they would be keeping them as prisoners, but that's what we need to find out,' Cara replied.

'We've been here before,' Simran said. 'There's no way we can get anywhere near Hartfield Manor. It's a suicide mission.'

'Maybe not.' Cara looked at Emma.

A trickle of fear skittered across Emma's skin as she comprehended what Cara was suggesting. 'What do you need me to do?'

'We only need to look inside that facility,' Cara said. 'No fighting, no grand gestures, no heroics. You have Amelia's face. Nobody at Hartfield would stop you from walking up the main drive and through the front door.'

'Are you crazy?' Dylan jumped up from his seat. 'You can't ask her to walk into that place.'

Cara sighed. 'I'm not. I want her to sneak on-site to reconnoitre the grounds and those outbuildings *without* being seen. But if someone did happen to cross her path, she could pretend to be her sister.'

'It's okay, Dylan.' Emma was grateful for his support. 'I'll do it.'

'You won't be alone,' Cara added. 'Kai will go with you. If anyone gets close to you, he can distort their senses and give you time to escape.'

'We'll go tonight,' Kai said to Emma. 'It'll be okay. I'll make sure of it.'

Emma was relieved that she didn't have to go on the mission alone. Having Kai with her was a blessing. He was strong and dependable—the boulder that stood at the centre of the group as everyone else streamed around him like water in a raging river.

'Get some sleep.' Cara broke into Emma's thoughts. 'Kai and Emma leave at dusk.'

'What about the rest of us?' Simran asked. 'What's our mission?'

Cara shifted on her feet, and everyone stopped moving to watch her. It was an unnatural action for Cara. She was the leader—the one they relied on—but her demeanour told a different story.

'We need to stay behind and cover for them,' said Cara.

'Cover for them? Why?' asked Simran.

'You all know Joey is under the Haven's radar. We've kept it that way for years, and I never want to jeopardise his safety, but when he gives us information like this, it's worthy of further investigation. James didn't see it like that.'

'You told James about Joey!' Simran gasped.

Cara said, 'I told him one of our sources gave us the information. I didn't give him any names, but he said no to any missions. We all need to stay in the bunker, at least for the time being.'

'And you disagree.' Emma felt torn between her loyalty to Cara and her growing feelings for James.

'We need answers, Emma. *You* need answers. The Hartfield family are moving their pieces into position,' said Cara.

'It's likely that Amelia awoke your Dhampir side for more than a freaky family reunion,' Jess said with a shrug.

She was right. They both were. They needed more answers, so that they would be prepared for anything the Immortal family threw at them. If Amelia's appearance was only the start of this, Emma dreaded what might come next.

'So Kai and I sneak out on this mission, and you stay behind and pretend we're in bed with the flu or something. What then?' Emma asked.

'Find out what's going on at Hartfield Manor, then we can approach the Haven leaders with all the facts. If we know what we're facing, we've got a better chance of surviving whatever is coming.'

Emma was satisfied that this tiny rebellious action would not have an impact on what she hoped to have with James and nodded her consent. 'We leave at dusk.'

'Dusk,' Kai repeated.

They filed off into their bedrooms to get some well-deserved rest, but Emma's mind was a swirling mass of thoughts and feelings. Her kiss with James now seemed like a distant memory, yet his scent still lingered on her skin and clothes. She ran her fingers across her lips, remembering the feel of his against hers.

'You okay?' Jess's voice broke through the silence in their bedroom. 'You seem…different.'

'I'm fine, Jess. It's been crazy over the last few days.'

'I know, but—'

'But what?' Emma propped herself up on her elbow, so she was facing her friend. Simran climbed out of her bed and sat on the end of Jess's. They looked like they were staging an intervention.

'Your aura,' Jess said. 'It's flaring in beautiful streams of red and pink.'

Emma sat up, crossed her legs, and rested her back against the wall. 'What does that mean?'

'If I didn't know any better, I'd say you were in love,' Jess said.

Emma stared at Jess for a long moment. There was no hiding from vampire powers.

'You know you can talk to us, Em,' Simran said. 'We're family now, remember?'

'I don't know what to say,' Emma said quietly. 'I've never experienced anything like what I'm feeling right now. I'm not sure what to do about it.'

'Start by telling us who it is you've got feelings for,' Simran said. 'I'm an expert in people-to-people interactions and can tell you straight away if they're worth pursuing.'

'That's right,' Jess added. 'She warned me off Katie, but I didn't listen and look how that turned out!'

'I didn't warn you off the girl. I told you to be careful, that's all. She has a needy vibe, and I didn't want you getting sucked in.'

Jess giggled. 'See? We have our very own relationship guru at our beck and call.'

Simran laughed and took a bow.

'It's James,' Emma said softly, almost hoping the girls hadn't heard her above their laughter and teasing.

She was wrong. They had both heard.

Jess tipped her head to the side, and her eyes widened. Simran's fingers momentarily fluttered to her lips, hiding a tiny smile.

'Isn't he like a thousand years old or something?' Simran said.

It was Emma's turn to laugh. 'I didn't realise age mattered in the vampire world!'

'Oh, I didn't mean it like that. It's just he…he is…he has—'

'He's the head of the Haven,' Jess said. 'You can't expect him to return any affection you feel, and I'd hate for you to get hurt.'

'It might be a bit late for that,' Emma mumbled.

Both girls shot off Jess's bed to sit beside Emma.

'There was a spark of something when we did the mind-meld, but I brushed it off. I thought the same as you, Jess. He's the head of the Haven and wouldn't notice me beyond being the newbie vamp, but he did notice me. He did more than notice me. He's watched out for me, supported me, and tonight, he kissed me.'

Silence.

Simran and Jess glanced at one another and then back to Emma. Their faces were expressionless, not divulging any of their thoughts or judgements.

'Did you kiss him back?' Jess asked.

'Uh-huh!'

They burst out laughing at the same time, and Emma couldn't help the smile that pulled at the corner of her mouth. She rolled her eyes as her friends continued to snort and cry with laughter.

'What's so funny?' Emma asked.

'Nothing,' Simran gasped. 'It's brilliant! You've been a vampire for less than a heartbeat, and you've already bagged yourself a hottie vampire who is not only our leader, but is in a position to give you everything you've ever wanted. And they call *me* the siren!'

Emma laughed until tears spilled down her cheeks, until her sides ached, and until they all fell back onto their own beds exhausted.

She had taken an enormous step forward by opening up and being vulnerable. It felt good.

'Sweet dreams, Em,' Jess whispered into the darkness. 'We won't tell the guys. Not yet. Let's see how everything plays out before you start wearing that big pink flaming aura of yours on your sleeve.'

'Thanks, both of you. I'm so glad you came into my life.'

'Same here,' Simran said. 'We're here for each other now and for all eternity.'

9

Kai and Emma awoke early and slipped out before anyone in the bunker saw them. They couldn't risk using the cage to Dustin's cottage and putting their friend in danger, so they used the fire escape, tunnel, and staircase they had taken the day Amelia had attacked.

It seemed like it had happened such a long time ago. Emma still hadn't plucked up the courage to speak to Flora. Her grandmother-who-wasn't-her-grandmother had been given a secluded room to use for her recuperation until she was strong enough to return to Allendale. She had asked to see Emma, but Emma was not ready to hear all the gruesome details of her betrayal face-to-face yet.

'When we get to the surface, we need to borrow Dustin's car,' Kai said, breaking into her musings.

'Borrow? You mean steal!'

'Yes, that's exactly what I mean. Dustin isn't going anywhere since he's still recovering, so we may as well use it to get as close as we can to Hartfield Manor.'

Emma chuckled. She loved the way her friends justified what they did in the simplest of terms. No wonder they were the elite nest with the most topside missions. They did what they had to do to get the job done, and they lived by their own set of rules.

'Can we trust Joey's information?' Emma suddenly wondered why a rogue vampire's message had carried so much weight.

'Joey is a good guy. We can trust him. He wasn't always a rogue vamp, so he understands the way the Haven operates.'

'Really? He lived at the Haven?'

'Yes, before I joined. He was on duty the night the bunker was attacked, and Henric partly blamed him. He banished Joey knowing full well that he would be sending one of his nests to destroy him. Cara's nest was chosen, but she couldn't do it. She told Henric the mission was a success and protected Joey by taking him to the moors where he stood half a chance of surviving.'

'Cara went against Henric's orders! Wow, I never thought she would do something like that. She's always so devoted.'

'She *is* devoted. She's the most loyal nest leader you'll ever meet, but she's also compassionate and remembers what it was like to be human. Some of the vamps in that bunker bury their humanity the second they arrive, but she never did.'

'She taught you how to survive in the same way.' It was more of a statement than a question, as Emma had seen the evidence for herself.

'Staying in touch with your human side keeps you sharp. It makes you a better vampire in my opinion. How are we supposed to shield the humans from rogues if we can't understand the way they work, feel, or think?'

They arrived at the staircase, and Emma followed Kai in silence, mulling over their conversation. Henric had come across as cold and out of touch at their initial meeting. He was nothing like James, yet here she was on a mission that went against James's orders. Cara seemed to be making a habit of rebelling against the leaders no matter their style of leadership. Still, Emma could not find any reason to disagree with Cara's decisions.

Kai lifted the hatch, and they broke out into the cold air. The sun had set, and the black sky was beginning to fill with stars before night truly fell and two hundred vampires awoke. They needed to be far away before any of the vamps started venturing out on missions or errands.

Through the cottage window, Emma saw Pierce moving around the living room. His nest had been placed on guard duty to make sure Dustin and the gateway to the bunker were protected against further attacks. She hadn't seen Dustin since they had shipped him off in the back of an ambulance, and she was eager to check up on the big man. Amelia had beaten him, broken his ribs, and left him for dead. Somewhere deep inside of her, Emma felt responsible for her sister's actions. She knew Dustin wouldn't see it that way, but she still wanted to apologise.

Dustin's old car was parked to the left of the cottage, nestled under a wooden structure to protect it from the inclement weather that battered the North. The keys were in the ignition, which gave Emma hope that Dustin was helping them in his own way.

'We need to move it out to the road,' Kai said in a hushed tone.

They rolled the car down the drive until they arrived at the road, which was far enough away from the cottage that Pierce and his crew would think it was a passing car. Kai fired up the engine, and they disappeared into the night, following the tiny, twisty country lanes deeper into the countryside.

'Dylan showed me a spot on the blueprints where we should be able to gain access to the grounds without being seen or coming face-to-face with any of the Hartfield goons—no offence.'

'I might be a Hartfield, but I'm not a goon!'

Kai grinned over at her. 'I know. I don't want you to think being a Hartfield makes you any less of a friend.'

'Thanks. That means a lot. It's all a bit strange to be honest. All my life I've been Emma Hartfield, the loner girl from Allendale. It was just a name that belonged to my parents and was scribbled on a birth certificate. Little did I know it had such a deadly legacy.'

'You're your own person, Emma. No name will ever take that away from you. That loner girl from Allendale is pretty cool, and I don't care about your name.'

'You did though. All of you did. When you first found out that I was a Hartfield, you were as freaked out as everyone else. So what's changed?'

'Nothing has changed. We got to see who you are. We appreciated that you were nothing like the Hartfield family who have terrorised the Haven and the half-bloods for years. I guess it took us by surprise when you announced it that night.'

'It took *me* by surprise to discover I was part of something so evil. When I saw the pictures on the computer that night in the rec room, I couldn't believe it.'

'What pictures?'

Emma took a deep breath. No more secrets, no more holding back.

'On one of my first nights in the Haven, I struggled to get to sleep. I went for a walk through the halls and found a computer left on in the recreation room. I thought someone was researching something and had left before I arrived, but the web page was open on information about Hartfield Manor. It was the first time I put two and two together.'

Out of the corner of her eye, Emma saw Kai's fingers tighten on the steering wheel. He tensed and narrowed his eyes as if mulling over what his response should be.

'Sounds to me like someone in the bunker wanted, or needed, you to find it,' Kai said.

'That's what I thought. I knew someone was watching me. I hadn't discovered my vampire power yet, so it was just a creepy sensation rather than knowing I was being watched.'

'If it was planted there for you to find, then someone other than Henric, the council, and us knows who you are. Either that or one of the leaders wanted you to find out.'

'James,' Emma said quietly.

'He helped you find out about Amelia and what happened to your mum, so it makes sense that he could be the one who would want you to know your heritage.'

'Maybe. It feels like the kind of thing James would do, but why not talk to me? Why leave it out like a cryptic clue? It feels more like a single breadcrumb from a trail I haven't found yet.'

'Who knows? James has his own secrets. Perhaps he likes playing games with people.'

Emma's shoulders stiffened at Kai's words. 'What secrets?'

Kai shrugged as if it wasn't important, but Emma couldn't let it go.

'If he's keeping something from me, then I need to know, Kai. I've been letting him inside my brain, and I need to know it's safe.'

She didn't mention their kiss, but the rising panic at Kai's words filled her thoughts.

'I'm sure he's fine. I'm probably reading something from nothing. I just get a vibe from the guy, like he's watching us for a school project.'

She recalled her brief chat with James in the recreation room in the bunker. He had spoken to her but had never taken his eyes off the room. She had brushed it off as him playing at being the headmaster and keeping a wary eye on the pupils.

'It's his job to keep us all safe.' Emma tried to quell the bubble of fear that was churning in the pit of her stomach.

'I know. Forget I said anything.'

Emma stared into the black sky, hoping that she hadn't made a mistake by falling for James.

After a short drive, Kai pulled the car to a stop down a dirt track. 'We walk from here.'

Without any streetlights, it was challenging to navigate the field as they waded through mud and weeds. The faint shimmer of lights in a farmhouse served as a beacon on the horizon as they trudged west. Emma followed Kai as he crossed the uneven ground, using the deep grooves left by a tractor to create a path.

Nothing stirred in the shrubbery, and no nocturnal sounds filled the air. Everything was silent as they approached a ten-foot-high brick wall covered in climbing vines.

'Welcome to Hartfield Manor,' Kai whispered, pointing at the wall.

The walls ran left and right, snaking in a slight curve around what must have been the extensive grounds of the manor. Emma had seen the photographs and the aerial plans of the house and knew it was a massive area. Finding the exact spot where they needed to scale the wall was paramount to the success of their mission.

Kai veered off to the right and walked along the perimeter of the wall for a hundred yards before dropping his rucksack to the ground and taking out the rope they had packed.

'Ready?'

Emma nodded as he felt along the wall for something. A loose brick fell to the ground as his hand skimmed the surface, and he smiled.

'We can get over the wall here.' His voice was so low Emma had to lean in to hear him properly. 'A tree in a recent storm damaged the top of the wall. They haven't repaired it yet, so it's not as high. Joey's first piece of information is spot on, so let's see what else he was right about.'

They scaled the wall and dropped silently into the shrubbery beyond. In the distance, the imposing structure of the manor rose before them, and Emma took a moment to marvel at its beauty. This was the house her father had lived in, her mother had visited, and probably where her sister now resided. Guards patrolled the entrance, denying access to anyone other than the Immortal family themselves.

James had explained how her family were Immortal as they sat and watched the sleepy town below them the previous night.

Her grandfather had been human and had fallen in love with a beautiful temptress over a millennium ago. They had lived within a community that believed cannibalism held mystical powers and had developed a craving for blood as their only sustenance. Five such tribes had existed, surviving off the flesh and blood of their victims. The five tribes became the Immortal families. One by one, they came to Briton and continued practising their evil ways, murdering their way across the land.

As if cursed for the way they lived, the females of the family began to die, leaving the men without any form of reproducing. With no wives to care for them, they became more feral. Their powers developed until hundreds of years later they were no longer human. They were trapped in limbo, ageing at a fraction of the time it should have taken.

Emma remembered reading about a dreadful accident which had caused the death of Edward Hartfield, her grandfather. Still, she knew that he could not have died in any fictional accident. As an Immortal, he had to be beheaded, burned, and buried in a graveyard to die—another side effect of their bloodthirsty existence.

It was the Immortal families' fault the world was full of vampires. They waged war on the half-bloods they had created and began a desperate attempt to create more Dhampirs—female Immortals—by mating with humans.

Emma felt sick thinking about it. Her mother, her sweet and beautiful mother, had been a young girl when she had fallen for a handsome boy with sandy blond hair. He had played his part to perfection, making sure she fell in love with him. He'd even convinced her to marry him in some bizarre show of loyalty. Had she known what he was? It plagued Emma's thoughts. Had she believed the twin girls she carried were the result of a normal, healthy relationship with a normal boy? Or was she a willing participant in their macabre experiment? It pained her that she may never know.

'The outbuildings are this way,' Kai said, interrupting Emma's train of thought as he motioned off to his right.

'Let's get this over with then.'

She took one last look at the manor before turning her back and following Kai through the darkness.

The buildings were single storey with interconnecting corridors and a flat roof. Narrow windows ran along the top of the walls, allowing light to flood the interior without allowing anyone to see outside.

Each building had a lantern skylight with four panels of glass covered in years of grime.

No guards patrolled this area, which Emma thought was strange. A prisoner block should always be secured. It was oddly quiet.

'Let's climb up.' Kai gestured to the roof. 'We might get a better look through the skylight.'

They inched up the drainpipe and crawled across the flat roof until they were able to see through the glass. Emma used the edge of her sleeve to rub a hole in the dirt and peered into the space below.

'Let's see what's going on,' Kai murmured, rubbing at his own patch of glass.

The outbuilding was kitted out with rows of beds and sets of drawers. There were about fifty beds in total, and Emma wondered if the same setup applied to the other outbuilding. About twenty vampires milled around the space, chatting, playing cards, or reading books and magazines. It looked more like a hostel than a prison.

The door at the end of the building opened, and Amelia stalked in followed by two burly vampires. Emma flattened herself to the roof, convinced her twin would sense her presence even if she couldn't see her.

'Phase one is underway, and your colleagues should be finished by now. We thank you for your cooperation.' The gathered vampires cheered at Amelia's words. Emma and Kai exchanged a questioning look.

'You get to rest for a few more days before we start phase two, so make the most of your time off. If it's revenge you want, then you'll get it,' Amelia said.

More cheers arose as Amelia turned and left the building, leaving the door ajar as she went. Kai's brow wrinkled as he scrutinised the group of vampires below them.

'What is it?'

'They have weapons.' Kai motioned to a stash of crossbows piled on one of the beds. 'These vamps aren't being held against their will. I recognise some of these guys. They're old Haven residents—ones that Henric banished.'

'What are you saying?'

Kai took a deep breath and rolled away from the skylight, inching toward the drainpipe. He dropped to the ground silently. Emma followed. That bubbling sensation of fear returned as she ran after Kai.

Once back in the farmer's field, she grabbed at his arm, bringing him to an abrupt halt. 'What's going on?'

'We have to return to the Haven.' He bit his bottom lip. 'Joey got it wrong. They're not taking these vampires as prisoners. They're building a half-blood army.'

They didn't speak all the way back to Dustin's cottage. Kai drove like a maniac through the tiny country lanes, and his anxiety poured from him in waves. Emma's mind spun with what-ifs.

What if these vampires attacked Dustin again? What if they did more than break a few ribs and leave him battered and bruised? What if Pierce and his nest became victims of phase one too?

• • •

The cottage was dark when they arrived save for the single lamp Dustin always left on in the small window by the front door. They hadn't bothered to roll the car down the drive this time; this wasn't the time for secrecy. Kai's face seemed paler somehow as they stowed the vehicle under the wooden structure and rushed to the front of the cottage.

They barrelled through the front door to find Pierce stretched out on the sofa. Katie was sitting on the floor playing with the cat, and the other members of Pierce's nest were scattered throughout the living space, reading or chatting amongst themselves.

'Jeez! Kai, you nearly gave me a heart attack,' Pierce yelled as he jumped to his feet. 'Where's the fire?'

Kai didn't stop to chat; he flew across the room and pulled back the bookcase to reveal the cage. Smoke billowed out from the opening as a burning smell permeated the room.

'What's going on?' Dustin stood in the doorway of his bedroom, dressed in flannel pyjama bottoms and a white T-shirt. The bandages around his body poked through the fabric. The bruises on his face were raw, and Emma swallowed a sudden desire to cry. He stood there, staring as Emma raced across the room.

'Phase one!' Kai and Emma said together.

'I was only joking about the fire!' Pierce said as he grabbed Dustin's ID card and swiped it across the panel. Kai yanked the cage door open and stepped inside. Emma followed with Pierce one step behind.

'Stay with Dustin. We'll report back as soon as we know what's happening,' Pierce said to his nest before closing the cage door.

The light in the lift flickered on and off as they descended into thick smoke. Whatever had happened in the bunker was bad. Emma suppressed her rising bile.

'We heard nothing in the cottage,' Pierce said as the cage clattered to a halt. 'No alarms, no shouts, no messages.'

The long hallway was encased in darkness as they hugged the wall and made their way to the main doors. Pierce was right; the alarms that had sounded when Dustin was attacked were silent. Nobody rushing about. Only smoke and silence.

'What are we expecting to find through those doors, Kai?' Pierce stopped them with a raised hand, and his brow creased as he glanced between Kai and the double doors that led to the main bunker.

'The Immortals have created a half-blood army, and this'—he waved around at the black smoke and eerie silence—'is just the start.'

Pierce moved aside with a nod, and Kai inched the door open. Thinking about what they might find made Emma feel like her head was going to explode. If the vampires from Amelia's phase one had infiltrated the bunker, then they had to have come in through one of the secret tunnels. The main entrance in Dustin's cottage hadn't been disturbed. Someone inside the Haven had given away information.

Henric's banished vampires were never meant to live very long in the outside world. That was why he sent the nests out after them.

Perhaps Cara's empathic nature had been the undoing of them. Emma wondered again about Joey's involvement in this. As an ex-resident, he would know the whereabouts of all the Haven's secret entrances. Would he give that information away if the price was right or his life was in danger?

Kai seemed satisfied that the area was safe and shoved the door wide to give Emma and Pierce their first look at the carnage beyond. Small fires raged at various points along the corridor to their right. Smoke swirled across the ceiling, looking for an escape route. Red bulbs flashed intermittently.

The recreation room to their left was in total disarray. The computers had been ripped from the walls and lay smashed in pieces across the floor. Chairs were upturned and tables obliterated, but the single most disturbing aspect of the scene was the red mist that covered everything.

Dead vampires.

Dotted throughout the debris were injured vampires, groaning and moving carefully. Their faces shone red in the flickering emergency lighting.

'What the hell—' Pierce launched into action, sprinting to the nearest vampire, a young boy who was impaled on a chair leg. Fortunately, the wooden implement had missed his heart and was wedged in his stomach, otherwise he would have been another red stain on the carpet.

'What happened?' Emma knelt beside Pierce and the boy to help extract the wooden leg. She knew what had happened but needed to hear it for herself.

'There was no alarm, no warning,' the boy said. 'They were so methodical, moving through the rooms and killing anyone they found.'

Emma glanced back at Kai, who was staring off toward the door that led to the sleeping quarters. The same thought must have crossed his mind. Were Cara, Dylan, Jess, and Simran still alive?

'They knew what they were doing,' the boy continued. 'Like they'd been here before and knew every square inch of the place.'

'Where's Henric?' Pierce asked. 'Are the council leaders safe?'

Emma's head snapped up at his words. She hadn't even thought about James, or Flora for that matter. Both of them would have been in the area assigned to the council leaders.

'My grandmother?' Emma's voice cracked as she said the words. Flora was human—the only human in the bunker. The invading horde could have done far worse to her than a stake to the heart.

The boy shook his head. 'I'm sorry. I don't know what happened with Henric or your grandmother. They were organised and were purposeful about who they targeted.'

'What do you mean?' Kai asked.

'They specifically chose who to kill and who to hurt. It was like they had a list telling them who was supposed to die, and I was one of the lucky ones.'

Pierce helped the boy to his feet and propped him against the wall before looking around the recreation room for more injured victims to help.

'Go,' Pierce said, addressing Emma and Kai together. 'Find Cara and your nest. I'll look for survivors and meet you b—'

They both sprinted for the door before Pierce had finished his sentence.

Most of the doors in the sleeping area were either open or hanging from the hinges. As they approached number seven, panic rose in the pit of Emma's stomach. The what-ifs began to surface again, and her steps faltered.

'You okay?' Kai asked.

'No, not even a little bit. Part of me needs to see it for myself, but the other part of me—'

'I know, but these are our friends. They might be hurt.'

He was right. Emma straightened her back and gave a sharp nod, confirming she was ready. The two of them stepped inside.

The room was shrouded in darkness. Broken glass and ceramics crunched beneath their shoes as they crossed the living room. Kai flipped the light switch in the kitchen area, and it flickered to life, casting a warm glow over their ruined belongings.

Everything had been overturned or broken, but there was no red mist on the walls or floor. Had they escaped before the carnage?

Kai slipped into the room he shared with Dylan and returned a few seconds later, shaking his head. He moved toward Cara's bedroom door as Emma approached the room she shared with the girls.

'Nothing here,' Kai called out.

Emma turned the handle and pushed open the door. The light was on, illuminating the bright red glow that covered the centre of the floor. She sank to her knees with a loud sob as Kai barrelled past her.

'Jess! Sim!'

A weak moan filled the air, and Emma leapt to her feet. She sidestepped the bloody puddle and yanked open the wardrobe doors. She let out a huge breath. Simran was lying on the floor inside with crossbow bolts buried in her thigh and arm. Her face was covered in blood from a deep cut above her eye.

'What happened?' Emma helped her friend as gently as she could, easing her from the wardrobe and guiding her to sit on the end of the bed.

Kai grabbed a towel, soaked it in the sink, and began to clean Simran's face. Her eyes were wide and shiny, and she scanned the room wildly. Emma looked around the room, trying to figure out what Simran was searching for, when her gaze settled on the red stain on the floor. Glancing back to Simran, Emma saw tears spilling down her cheeks as a loud sob escaped the girl's tiny frame.

'No! Jess!' Simran screamed. It took both Emma and Kai to restrain her as she launched herself off the bed, ripping the bolts from her limbs and sending a spray of blood across the floor to mingle with that of their friend. 'No!'

'I'm so sorry, Sim.' Kai wrapped his arms around her and held her tight.

She fought against him for a moment before her knees buckled, and they both crumpled to the floor. Simran sobbed hysterically into his shoulder as Emma lowered herself to sit beside them. The pain in her chest was like nothing she had ever felt before. Even her own death hadn't hurt this much.

Simran's sobbing began to subside, and the three of them sat on the floor in a silent huddle beside the place where their friend had been murdered.

'We were attacked. They had crossbows,' Simran managed to say.

Kai picked up the towel once again and began to clean her cut. She winced but carried on talking.

'The arrows hit me, and I fell hard. Jess pushed me inside the wardrobe while they reloaded. It happened so fast. I heard her scream, but then I must have blacked out.'

None of them could hold back their tears as they reflected on how Jess had sacrificed herself to save her friend.

'Have you seen Cara or Dylan?' Kai asked.

'No, I think Henric sent Dylan on a brief mission, but I don't know where and I haven't seen Cara since she told us to cover for you two.'

'There was a boy in the recreation room,' Emma said between her tears. 'He said they were intentionally killing some and injuring others.'

'It doesn't make sense,' Kai said. 'Why not wipe out the entire bunker? Why pick and choose who to murder?'

'Their strategy is to cause panic as each nest grieves their fallen friends,' Cara said. She stood in the doorway, staring at what remained of Jess. Her face was as hard as granite. 'They've taken out over half of the bunker, and I'm fairly certain they'll be back to finish the job soon.'

'Phase two!' Emma said. 'Joey was wrong about the vampire prisoners. They're not keeping them captive. They're using them to form an army.'

'Emma's right. We saw about twenty vamps talking to Amelia about phase two. She sent phase one last night and this'—he waved his hand around him—'is what they accomplished.'

'It was *your* sister who instigated this. *Your* family murdered our people—murdered Jess!' A muscle twitched in Simran's cheek as she spat the words at Emma. 'It's all *your* fault!'

Emma jumped back in surprise at the venom in her friend's voice. Simran glared at her with a murderous look in her eye.

'It's not my fault,' Emma gasped. 'I can't be held responsible for what the Hartfields do.' She spoke the words, but she didn't really believe them. Simran was right. If she hadn't come to the Haven, Dustin wouldn't have been hurt. Jess would still be alive.

'I think you should leave,' Kai said. His eyes told her that he didn't mean it in a bad way. He was sending her away to protect her from Simran's grief, but it hurt nonetheless.

She stood up, brushed past Cara, who didn't even look in her direction, and fled the room. Tears blurred her vision as she hurtled down the corridor toward the recreation room.

She crashed into Katie as she stumbled into the open space where Pierce had rounded up the injured vampires.

'Emma! Is everything okay?' The small girl grasped Emma's shoulders to steady her.

The sight of Katie's pale face triggered something inside Emma, and she sobbed. All she could think of was Jess and how much she and Katie had cared for each other. Another relationship destroyed because of her family.

'I'm so sorry, Katie. It's Jess. She's dead.'

Katie stared at her for a long time as if processing her words. Tears spilled over her cheeks as realisation dawned, but she brushed them away with the back of her hand.

Pierce slid his arm around Katie. 'Go. Say your goodbyes.'

Katie darted off toward number seven.

'I was under orders to keep my nest away from Cara's,' Pierce said quietly. 'Henric told me who you are after the attack on Dustin.

He thought having you here may endanger the Haven. I know it was harsh to keep Katie away from Jess, but I had to follow orders.'

'I'm sorry for what my family has done to you all,' Emma said with a gasp. The sheer magnitude of the situation hit her full in the chest. She felt like someone had split her open with a machete and left the wound raw and ragged.

'You've got the power to stop this.'

'How? How the hell can I stop an Immortal family?'

'Leave. Leave the Haven and go somewhere else—far away. Hopefully, they'll follow you, and we can rebuild in peace.'

He twisted on his heel and stalked away, leaving Emma reeling at the harshness of his words. Nobody wanted her here. Even her own friends had turned against her.

Maybe it was time to leave, but she had to find Flora first. She couldn't leave her here.

Emma set off running past the dazed and injured vampires, past the isolated fires, and past the blood that tarnished the walls. She didn't stop until she entered the open-plan office and James's apartment, which overlooked the space.

Her grandmother's private room was in the furthest corner, beyond the broken desks and the smashed glass. A deep-rooted fear washed over Emma as she picked her way over the rubble. What was she about to find? Another murder victim or a newly turned vampire?

The door was missing, and the room was trashed in much the same way as the rest of the bunker. Emma searched the entire room, but Flora was gone. Perhaps Amelia had decided to take Flora back, and her phase one disciples had kidnapped the old woman again.

Emma believed that her sister was playing a cruel game of cat and mouse. She didn't know what the end goal was, but if she had any hope of surviving the Hartfields, she had to learn to play the game or change the rules.

A noise behind her interrupted her thoughts, and she spun to see James helping Flora down the spiral staircase. Relief flooded her system as she saw both were safe.

'Emma!' Flora rushed forward, embracing her tightly. 'I'm so sorry I lied to you. I only did it to keep you safe.'

'I know,' Emma said, suddenly not as angry about the lies as she had been. 'It's okay. I understand.'

'James kept me hidden as those awful vampires swept through. We hunkered down and waited for them to leave.'

Flora looked older than she had the last time Emma had seen her. The feisty older woman who had scared the residents of Allendale was broken and almost timid in her mannerisms. Was it possible that they had reversed roles and Emma was now the strong one?

'Are you okay?' James's voice slid over her skin like a soothing balm.

'Jess is dead,' Emma stepped away from Flora. 'I haven't seen Dylan yet. He was sent out on a mission but Cara and the rest of the nest survived.'

He reached for Emma's hand and squeezed. 'I'm so sorry.' He tugged her closer until they were inches apart. 'What can I do to help?'

She melted into his arms as the tears fell freely. Her body shook as the grief overwhelmed her. Grief for her friend and grief for herself. She had achieved the impossible and found a family where she belonged, and now that family had been ripped away from her.

Nothing would ever be the same again.

10

'I don't want to leave you,' Flora said as Emma walked her to the waiting taxi. She was heading to the train station, and from there she would travel back to Allendale.

Emma did not know what would happen next. She had lost everything three times over, but making sure Flora was out of harm's way had become a priority.

'I know, but you're not safe here. If Amelia's phase two is anywhere near as brutal as phase one, then I want you at the opposite end of the country.'

'But what about you? Amelia's going to be coming for you, Emma.'

'I don't want you to worry about that. I'll deal with it.'

'The day your beautiful mother was killed was one of the hardest days of my life.' Flora's voice was so low it was almost a whisper. 'Maybe if there'd been enough time, I could have saved Amelia too. Everything happened so fast.'

It was the first time Flora had opened up about that day. They had chatted in short bursts about it over the last two days as James had kept them isolated in his rooms, but Emma had only wanted the facts, not the emotions.

'You couldn't have known that she survived.' Emma swung Flora's bag onto the back seat of the cab. 'Thomas murdered my mother in cold blood, and you did what any sane person would do. You ran.'

Flora cupped Emma's face in her hands and fixed her with the stern gaze that Emma had known and loved all her life. It was something the old Flora used to do—the one who ripped up rule books and berated local policemen.

'Your mother was one of the strongest women I ever met, and I see that strength inside you. Don't let them win. Family isn't always blood. Sometimes the people you surround yourself with become a sturdy anchor that keep you from getting lost in the storm.'

'I think it's too late for me to find that now.' Emma had tried to speak with Cara and Kai but had been unsuccessful. Simran had refused to see her, and Dylan hadn't yet returned from the mission that had kept him out of the Haven during the attack. 'Whatever happens next will be between my sister and me.'

'You can't take the Hartfields on by yourself. After your mother told me what Thomas was, I studied him. I researched the family and learned as much as possible about vampires. I wanted to be prepared, but none of that knowledge equipped me for how evil that family could be. Find a way back to your friends. Rebuild that trust and you'll stand a chance.'

'I've tried. They're not interested.'

'Emma, I love you. God knows I love you as much as any real grandmother would. We might not be blood-related, but you're my family. I believe in you. All your life, you've isolated yourself, and I never said anything. Part of me hoped it was a phase, but the other part of me knew that the Dhampir gene lay dormant inside you.

'You pulled away from everyone and lost yourself in this dark cloud, and I get it. Trust me. I saw your mother do the same thing. You're not just a human girl coping with an impossible situation. You're as much human as you are vampire. You're special.'

Emma's eyes filled with tears as she listened to the woman who had raised her as her own for nearly eighteen years. Nobody had asked her to take on such a role, but she'd done it anyway, to honour a young woman who'd left a remarkable legacy.

'You've struggled with that darkness all your life, but I could never tell you why you felt the way you did,' Flora continued. 'Maybe it's time you embrace that part of yourself and fight darkness with darkness.'

She kissed Emma on the cheek and climbed into the taxi, closing the door behind her. Her sad smile was the last thing Emma saw as the car drove off into the distance.

• • •

Standing outside Dustin's cottage, Emma watched the empty driveway until her head started to ache. She hadn't fed enough yesterday, and the early morning sunshine was pulling at her. She turned away from the road and went back inside the cottage, back to her vampire life, and back into the cloud of darkness.

Dustin was waiting for her as she closed the door.

'Here you go, princess. Thought you might need some breakfast.'

He handed her a mug of blood and motioned for her to sit on the sofa. The inside of the cottage was back to normal following the recent attacks, and Dustin's cat had returned to its usual spot in front of the fire.

'Why does life have to be so hard?' she said, not necessarily meaning it as a question but as more of an observation.

Dustin chuckled. 'Life is what you make it. If you want a hard life, then you'll go out and make one by telling yourself it's always that way. But if you want a life full of fun, love, and hope, then you'll do everything you can to make that happen instead.'

'How? It's not like you can snap your fingers and suddenly everything is great and your friends are your friends again.'

'No, it takes work and a whole lot of vulnerability, but it's worth it in the end.'

'I'm not sure I believe that.'

Dustin sat on the sofa next to Emma and cradled his mug of tea between his big hands. He had recovered slower than he had hoped and was still stiff and sore, but his duty as Revenant had kept him fighting his way back to good health.

'I've seen many youngsters come through this cottage over the years. All of them were broken in some way, but they had a common link that ended up being their strongest weapon. They were survivors, and you've survived more than most, princess.'

'I might have survived, but I've also managed to drive everyone away in the process.'

Emma didn't think any of Dustin's motivational words were going to fix her problems. Not today, not ever.

'I need to show you something.' Dustin stretched over the arm of the sofa and retrieved a leather-bound book the size of a breeze-block. 'This is the Vampire Codex. It contains the vampire origins and snapshots of vampire settlements throughout history.'

'James told me how vampires were created.' She sat up a little straighter at the sight of the ancient tome that contained information about her ancestors. 'He told me about how my grandfather fell in love with a tribal woman and became a cannibal.'

'That's true. I'd heard the old tales from my predecessor. I'd even read the entries that Henric and the other council leaders had added over the years, but I'd never read the entire thing properly. It hadn't occurred to me to read it in any capacity other than as part of my job. But after I met you, I decided to read it from a personal perspective.'

His eyes glinted in that excitable way they did when he knew something.

'What did you find?'

'There are entries from all the Immortal families, including snippets of how they lived, areas they ruled over, and the experiments they attempted.'

'Experiments? You mean like how they tried to create Dhampirs?'

'Yes, the notes go back centuries. Every family has their own interpretation and record of failures, but they never gave up. It was gruesome, reading some of the records. Not all of these women were treated the same way your mother was.'

'Who recorded everything? I thought the Immortal families competed with each other. Surely, they wouldn't have written everything in one book?'

'The records started hundreds of years ago when a Revenant kept detailed archives of each family. He would interview them and then transcribe everything into this Codex. Once the Haven was founded, it became the property of the council and kept in the care of yours truly and the other Revenants who came before me. Here's the interesting thing though—someone continued to keep the Codex updated, and it includes your birth and death.'

'What? How is that possible?'

'Henric was always aware of your existence, princess. He reads the Codex like I read a novel at bedtime. The race to create a Dhampir is referred to over and over, and it wouldn't have taken Henric long to track you down once he discovered Charlotte's name.'

'If Henric knew about me, why didn't he take me away from Flora when I was a baby?'

'You were human. He wouldn't have risked bringing a baby into the Haven with so many vampires, but he did have you watched over the years. When you died, he sent Cara out looking for you, even if he wasn't happy about bringing you into the safety of the Haven. He knew the importance of keeping you away from your family.'

'Keep me away from the Hartfield family? Why?'

Dustin opened the book and flipped the creamy pages until they fell open at one covered in intricate calligraphy.

Emma ran her finger over the words, following the deep sweep of the curly font. The faded writing was many years old and talked about the power of the Dhampir. It told of their legacy to bring about the destruction of the half-bloods and to restore the Immortal families to supreme power.

As she read about a prophecy buried in the cannibalistic ways of her ancestors, Emma began to understand why she had always felt so full of blackness and shadow. It was the way of the tribe. They believed that power came from the dark of night and unity. The union between a human and a vampire would create the necessary symmetry to spawn the ultimate authority.

It was outdated nonsense, but Emma sensed how strongly her ancestors had believed in the ability to conquer the world through their Dhampir creations. No wonder every Immortal family had tried to achieve this goal. Despite the horrors of the story, Emma couldn't help but feel an immense sense of pride that her mother was the one to do it.

She turned the page to discover fresh, crisp ink. The calligraphy gave way to a more modern scrawl.

At the top of the page, four words in bold jumped out at her. Icy tendrils climbed up Emma's spine as she rolled the words over and over in her mind.

The sisters will prevail.

She glanced up at Dustin, who was watching her.

'Me and Amelia?'

'Yes, I think so. Your mother was the only human that we know of to survive giving birth to a Dhampir, but she also managed to have twin girls. The belief systems of the Immortal families are strongly linked to unity, and you can't get more unified than twins.'

'Are you saying that the two of us will bring about the destruction of all half-blood vampires? If this is true, then it *is* my fault Jess is dead. It's *all* my fault.'

'It's only if you let it be true, princess. Do you want to destroy the Haven? Do you want to kill your friends?'

'Of course I don't!'

'Then do something different. Change these beliefs and show the Immortal families that they're wrong.'

'How?'

'I'm afraid I don't have that answer, princess. Just know that I'm here for you and will support anything you decide to do.'

Emma rubbed her hands across her face and let out an exasperated sigh. 'I've never felt so alone, Dustin.'

'You're not alone, not here. Cara and the guys will come around. They're grieving at the moment. You need to show them how much you care about what happens to them.'

The cottage door crashed open, and Dylan burst through, dragging a weaselly-looking boy dressed from head to foot in black behind him.

'What have we got here?' Dustin asked in his deep, booming voice. He stood up to his full height, towering over the new arrival with menace.

'Found him up a tree in your front garden. It appears he's been sent here to watch our movements,' Dylan said.

'Is that a fact?' asked Dustin.

The boy shook uncontrollably as he wrung his hands and fidgeted from foot to foot.

'Who sent you?' Dustin shouted at him.

'I…I can't say.'

'Was it Amelia?' Emma asked, closing the Codex and sliding it out of view.

The boy's eyes grew wide as he stared at Emma.

'Oh, yes. She's my twin sister. Same face, different personalities.'

'They told me you were a killer,' the boy muttered. 'You murder vampires like you're some warped bounty hunter.'

'Me? I've never killed a vampire in my life. Oh, wait…Yes, I did, but that was in self-defence.'

Dustin crossed his arms over his broad chest and shook his head. 'She calls it self-defence, but we know better. She kills vampires who don't cooperate.'

Emma gaped at her friend until she realised that he was using the fear this boy had of her against him.

'All my kills have been in self-defence.' She was getting into the swing of her new role as the evil twin. 'When fifty vampires attack you, what's a girl expected to do?'

'You killed fifty vampires?' If the boy had any colour in his cheeks, it would have drained away now.

'Oh no, I've killed *thousands*, but those fifty tried to attack me at the same time.'

'She didn't agree with the odds.' Dustin winked in her direction.

'I was only sent to watch the cottage,' the boy squealed. 'They wanted to know when he got back, so Amelia could start phase two.' He pointed at Dylan.

'Why are they interested in me?' Dylan asked.

'She said they all had to be together. All the nests had to be in the Haven. Otherwise, it was a waste of time,' the boy said.

'Amelia wants to break me by killing all my friends in one go,' Emma said. 'She needs me to crave revenge so I will give in to the darkness and become another heartless Hartfield monster.'

'We can't let her do that,' Dylan said.

Emma hesitated. Dylan hadn't been here for the attack and didn't know about Jess. She turned back to the boy.

'That girl you fight for is my evil twin. She sent her army here and killed over one hundred half-bloods just like you, including our best friend, Jess.'

Dylan looked at the ground, pinching the bridge of his nose. His expression darkened as he processed the news. Emma hated being the one to deliver the blow.

The boy whimpered. 'I don't know anything about that. I was just told to watch you.'

'I believe him,' Emma said. 'He can be of use to us.'

Dustin grabbed the boy by his hoodie and dragged him so close their noses almost touched. 'What is phase two?'

The boy shook as he hung limp in Dustin's big hands.

'To detonate a bomb and wipe out the Haven for good,' the boy said.

Dustin let the boy go, and he dropped to the floor like a stone.

'Bomb! They can't do that,' Dylan gasped.

'They already have,' said the boy between snivels. 'They left it behind during phase one. The attack was a distraction.'

'Oh my God. Dylan, we have to get everyone out of the Haven,' Emma said. Dread pooled in her stomach at the thought of what was hidden below their feet.

'You can't.' The boy sighed. 'I'm not the only one here to watch you. If anyone tries to leave, we have people outside waiting to pick everyone off as they come to the surface. All your secret entrances are covered. The only one we need to get outside is you.' He pointed at Emma.

She began to pace the floor as the horror of their situation rumbled around her mind. Everyone was in danger. Cara, Simran, Kai, James, and even Dustin. The blast would surely reach the cottage too.

'What should we do?' Dylan asked.

Emma said, 'We need to take this kid down to James. He'll know what t—'

A crossbow bolt shattered the lounge window and buried itself in the boy's heart. He exploded into fine red dust, coating everything in a two-metre radius. Emma, Dylan, and Dustin hit the floor.

'Looks like they didn't trust their little spy and with good reason,' Dylan said.

The three of them inched across the floor until they were alongside the bookcase and the hidden entrance beyond.

'If we go belowground now, there's a strong possibility we'll never get out alive,' Dylan said as they dragged the bookcase closed behind them and secured the cage door.

'It's the only option we have. There might be an entire army in the abbey ruins or dotted in the trees lining the road. We can't make a run for it this time,' Emma said.

'What do you suggest then?' Dylan asked.

Emma looked at Dustin, who gave her a big warm smile. He believed in her, and she knew that she had to start to believe in herself too.

'We need to work together in unity,' Emma said.

Dustin's smile grew bigger, and his rumbling laugh bubbled out.

'What's so funny?' Dylan asked, running his hands through his hair as he paced back and forth across the cage floor.

'Oh, nothing. I think our Dhampir has begun to understand her vampire powers.'

The two of them giggled, and Dylan shook his head.

'I don't see how sensing when someone is watching you can help us get out of this predicament,' Dylan said.

'Oh my God, Dylan! That's it! Amelia wants me alive, and they have orders to get me outside. If I go out first, I'll know exactly where they are thanks to my vampire gift. You're the fastest vampire here. Together we might be able to make a path and get everyone to safety before they detonate their bomb.'

'Shit! That might actually work.' Dylan laughed, his frown melting away.

'We'll talk to James and see if one of the secret entrances is a better option,' Emma said.

'Henric will know,' Dylan said. 'He's got a map of all the tunnels on his office wall.'

'I'm sorry, Henric didn't make it,' Dustin said. 'He was killed in the last attack. James is the only council leader left.'

Dylan slumped to the floor, squeezing his eyes shut. 'We have to end this.'

They made the rest of the trip in silence. Emma mulled over what they had already endured and what was still to come. When the cage finally came to a halt, there was an air of determination about their mission. They rushed through the Haven to James's apartment.

The spiral stairs vibrated as the three of them hurried up to the main door. James was already waiting for them at the top. The urgency of their steps must have roused him to investigate.

'We need your help,' Emma gasped. 'We have to get everyone out of the bunker as fast as we can.'

James listened intently to their tale as they explained about the bomb, the army outside the door, and the plan they had hatched. He remained impassive until they were finished and eagerly awaiting his response.

'Your plan is sound,' he said with a warm smile at Emma. 'Where do you plan to take us all?'

'I'm working on that,' Dustin said. 'It needs to be somewhere we can regroup before formulating our plan of attack.'

'Plan of attack? You intend to attack the Hartfield family?' James looked pointedly at Emma as he said it, and she faltered beneath his gaze.

'It's the only way.' She felt less confident with every minute. 'We can't let my sister get away with these murders. They killed Henric, Jess, and so many others. The Haven is supposed to be a sanctuary for half-bloods, but it's become a target.'

Dylan nudged Dustin as he moved toward the door. 'We'll start getting everyone ready to evacuate. You two can work on the logistics, and we'll meet in the rec room in an hour.'

They left Emma alone with James. She felt a flutter of annoyance that James had assumed she couldn't beat her sister.

'You're mad at me,' he said softly.

Emma began to walk around the room, absentmindedly picking up books and trinkets as she went. She was trying to distract herself from her mixed feelings. Was she mad at him, or was she just disappointed the man she loved hadn't been more supportive?

'I'm not mad. I guess I'm upset that you don't believe in me a bit more.'

He walked to her side and pulled her close, his lips inches from hers. 'I do believe in you. I know you have the strength to change everything.'

He leaned forward and gently kissed her neck, trailing his lips up and down the soft flesh between her ear and shoulder.

'We don't have time for this.' She wished the circumstances were different. She wanted time for this.

'I know,' he whispered. 'I can't help myself.'

She rolled her face to the side as he nuzzled her neck, and her gaze fell on the neat shelving unit and brightly coloured ornaments. Something tugged at her mind as she let her eyes wander around the bedroom.

Nothing was out of place. No gaps on the shelves, no ripped books, no piles of rubble. Everything was exactly as it had always been.

'Why didn't they destroy your room?'

'What?' James pulled away to look at Emma.

'Your room is perfect. Nothing is broken or torn. No carnage to be seen, unlike every other square inch of this place.'

'I guess they didn't think this space was important.'

He reached out to touch her, but she pulled away. Something felt wrong. She couldn't work out what it was, but the sensation was intense. Kai's words about James having secrets popped into her mind.

'Who are you?'

'You know who I am, Emma. What's going on? I thought you and I felt the same way about each other. Was I wrong?'

She shook her head, unable to deny the feelings that overwhelmed her every time James was close by.

'No, you're not wrong, but I have the strangest sensation that you're lying to me about something.'

'I would never lie to you. I love you.'

He said the words so softly Emma almost didn't catch them. His smile melted her heart, and she wanted to believe him more than anything. James drew her close and kissed her deeper than before, holding her tight.

As he pulled her toward him, her foot connected with something solid tucked beneath the bed, sending it sailing into the middle of the floor.

It took a while for Emma's eyes and brain to connect the dots, but there was no mistaking the device that now sat in full view. James hadn't noticed Emma's discovery as he had resumed kissing her neck.

Using small, gentle movements, Emma manoeuvred James until his back was against the wall. She stretched out her hand for the stone statue on his nightstand.

In one fluid movement, she swung the statue hard against the side of his head, knocking him unconscious.

There were no lights or numbers counting down on the bomb, and Emma hoped that meant it was inactive. She couldn't risk that James might be the one with the power to activate it. She ran down the spiral staircase to grab the heavy iron chains and a padlock she had seen in the operations centre. When she returned to James's room, she bound his hands and feet behind him. She knew the binding wouldn't hold him for long once he awoke. If she could get to Simran, maybe her friend could subdue him with her voice until they decided what to do.

Her heart screamed in pain as she glared down at James—the one who had betrayed them all.

It was beginning to make sense. James knew all the secret tunnels, and he had access to every inch of the Haven and its records, including the Codex. He had the knowledge and the authority to go unsuspected. His downfall was not allowing for Emma's inclination to overanalyse every tiny detail until it made sense to her.

The phase one vampires hadn't touched his room, because they knew he was their informant; instead, they used his place as a base to hide the bomb until it was needed.

James was the enemy within.

11

'What do you mean, you found the bomb?'

Cara stood in the rec room flanked by Dylan, Kai, and Simran. They stared at Emma as she explained her recent heartbreaking discovery.

'James is the one who let Amelia into the Haven.' The hole in Emma's chest ached more with every word. 'He was hiding the bomb in his room.'

'I don't believe it,' Kai said. 'I knew I sensed a weird vibe from the guy but not this. Never this.'

'Where is he now?' Cara's voice was clipped.

'I knocked him out and tied him up. He's in his room, but he won't be down for long. We need to secure him and find out what he knows. I thought Simran could use her gift to keep him docile.'

'And the bomb?' asked Cara.

Emma knelt and pulled open the satin sheet she had used to carry the weapon. The big black box had three wires looping from it into a smaller box with a digital clock face. Green and red buttons sat beside the clock, but neither was illuminated.

'I have no idea if it needs to be manually activated or if it can be done remotely. I don't think any of us should be around it to find out,' Emma said.

'Agreed,' Cara said. 'We need to get it out of the bunker and dismantle or detonate it in a safe space.'

She stalked off to speak to Pierce about what to do next. Without any council leaders to speak of, it was down to the nest leaders to rally the troops and make the big decisions.

'You knocked him out?' Simran said, addressing Emma for the first time since she had blamed her for Jess's death.

'Yes, and I chained him up.'

'That must have been difficult for you to do. Are you okay?'

A small weight shifted inside Emma's chest as Simran reached out and took her hand.

'I know how much you cared about him,' Simran added.

Emma's eyes filled with tears, but she refused to cry. This moment was about rejoicing and reuniting with her family. Even if it took one tiny step at a time, she would make it right.

'It hurt, but his betrayal hurt more.'

There was a commotion off to their right as two vampires from Pierce's nest pushed through carrying the chains Emma had used to restrain James. James was free.

'We need to go now!' Emma shouted, spurring everyone into action and pushing the swirling panic she felt aside.

'But which tunnel do we use?' Simran asked.

Emma surveyed the assembled vampires. There were less than sixty half-bloods left out of the two hundred, and all of them watched her with an expression of dread etched onto their faces.

'We go out the front door,' Kai said loudly so everyone could hear. 'We can fit twenty in the cage, so we will all be in Dustin's cottage in three trips. Emma will be able to gauge where Amelia's vampires are once she's outside.'

'Won't they kill her the minute she steps outside?' Simran asked.

'No, Amelia needs me alive,' Emma said.

Nobody pressed for further information. They followed Kai's instructions to the letter. Dylan went in the first load with Emma and Simran, while two vampires from Pierce's nest stayed behind to ensure there were no stragglers and no one got left behind.

'What are you going to do with the bomb?' Dylan asked when they arrived at the cottage. 'We can't risk it going off near the abbey ruins. There are hundreds of tourists out there.'

'Once everyone is clear we'll get it away from here. Maybe we should dump it on Hartfield Manor's doorstep!'

Dylan chuckled. 'Can you imagine if they blew up their own house thinking they were taking out the bunker? I'd pay to watch that.'

It was a snug fit in Dustin's cottage with everyone assembled for the grand escape. Emma positioned herself next to the front door with Dylan, Kai, and Simran by her side.

She turned to Dylan. 'When I sense where they are, I'll let you know first. You're our secret weapon. They won't know you've discovered them until it's too late. They'll be armed, so be careful. We only need to clear a pathway to get everyone through, okay?'

'Yeah, I'm good to go when you are.'

'It's time,' Emma said. 'Everyone ready?'

There was a soft chorus of acknowledgements as one by one the vampires prepared themselves for the race of their lives. Amelia had successfully pitched half-blood against half-blood in her war against the Haven, but Emma hoped today was the day only her sister's army perished.

The sun was low in the sky when Emma stepped outside. It wouldn't be long until sunset. Hopefully, the majority of the tourists would go home, leaving the area for the safety of their homes. Orange, red, and yellow streaked across the sky, silhouetting the abbey in a blaze of colour.

Emma turned her attention to the space around her. Clusters of people walked through the abbey grounds, but they posed no threat—humans out for a stroll. To her immediate right was the garage and an open field edged by a bramble hedge that ran along the length of the road. The long driveway cut through the grass lawn in front of her and was bordered by trees and hedges that met the road ahead. Open grassland sloped gently on her left toward Whitby Harbour in the distance.

The driveway provided their only cover, yet it also seemed the most obvious place to hide a potential army. Emma took a deep breath and concentrated on her surroundings.

Within seconds she sensed people watching her from the right. She closed her eyes and honed her inner sight until she could tell their exact location.

'There are five of them spaced evenly behind the brambles in the field on our right.' She spoke softly, directing her words through the crack in the door where she had left it ajar. 'I can also sense one lone vampire in the tree up ahead. I think he's the lookout.'

'He's mine.' Simran slipped a stake from her belt and nestled it in the palm of her hand.

'Dylan, you go on the count of three. Take out the first two. By the time you've done that, the rest of us will be right behind you.'

Emma stretched her arms to the sky as if limbering up in readiness for a run. Nobody but Dylan heard her counting, and on three, he burst from the cottage in a blur. He obliterated three of the waiting vampires before Emma and Kai could catch up.

Simran made quick work of the one in the tree with a clean throw of her stake. It was over in seconds. Cara ushered the group from the cottage toward the road and the farm building two fields away.

To the human eye, the building would look like a fuzzy impression on the horizon, but to Emma, it was the survival of everyone left from the bunker.

'We need to get rid of the bomb,' Dustin said when Emma, Kai, Simran, and Dylan returned to the cottage.

Emma had done a sweep, and nobody else was watching them. Only the five friends remained.

'Let me take it,' Dylan said. 'I can get to the shore the fastest and take a boat out to sea. If I can sink it, then it won't cause any damage even if it does detonate.'

Everyone looked at Emma.

'I can't make that decision,' Emma said with a short laugh. 'I'm just a newbie vamp with a crazy family and bad taste in men.'

Simran laughed, and the sound mended a small part of Emma's heart.

'Okay, I'll take charge if you're too scared to do it,' Kai teased. 'Dylan, take the bomb as far as you can and meet us back at the farm. We'll get Dustin to safety and check on Cara and Pierce.'

Before Kai had finished speaking, Dylan and the bomb were gone.

'Do I have to leave the cottage?' Dustin's face was a picture of misery.

'It's only until we decide what we're going to do about Amelia,' Kai said.

'And James,' Emma added. 'Let's not forget about the oldest vampire we know, who has details about every single one of us and also happens to be a traitorous snake.'

'We'll deal with James *and* Amelia,' Kai said. 'They'll both pay for what they've done to the Haven, and for what they did to Jess.'

● ● ●

The remaining half-bloods were under the care and protection of Cara and Pierce, who had taken control of the situation. They rallied their troops and assigned lookout missions and feeding runs. It was a well-executed process, and Emma couldn't help but think about how proud Henric would have been.

She hadn't warmed to the head of the council, but he had taken her in when she was vulnerable, despite his trepidation. The only way Emma could think of to thank or repay him was by avenging his death.

The sky was black as Emma walked down the 199 steps from the abbey to the harbour. She had slipped out unseen from the farm as she needed to clear her head. Before she realised it, she was on the cliff, standing beneath the whalebone arch.

Her nails dug into the palms of her hands as she stared at the bench where she and James had shared their first kiss. How had she missed it? She had always prided herself on being the silent observer who saw the way people manipulated others and remained untouched by the callous actions of others. Watching from a safe distance was how she had survived her dark thoughts all these years. Instead, she had let herself become the weak one and had fallen for someone who had betrayed them all.

A single tear trailed a path down her cheek, and she wiped it away with more aggression than was necessary. Mourning her loss wasn't going to solve their current predicament. Killing James, however, was one of the options open to the remaining Haven members.

Emma sat on the bench and peered out over the black expanse of the ocean. Her thoughts were a jumbled mess of whys and what-ifs, pain, and anger. She didn't sense the new arrival until he spoke.

'Hello, Emma.'

It wasn't a voice she recognised, yet she knew without a doubt who was sitting beside her. Part of her did not want to turn and face the man, but part of her had to know, had to see for herself. That part won.

The streetlamp behind them cast him in partial shadow. He leaned forward, exposing his facial features and the sandy blond hair that curled at the nape of his neck. The turned-up collar of his jacket framed his strong jawline. He was smiling, and Emma almost believed his smile was genuine. He sat with his hands clasped in his lap as if to give Emma the impression of submission, but she knew better. This man was dangerous; he was a murderer.

'What do you want, Thomas?'

'What? You don't feel comfortable calling me "Dad?"'

Emma laughed, but the sound was hollow and harsh. Every hair on her arms and neck stood on end. She did her best to remain calm, but her mind ran through all the available scenarios for escape.

She couldn't sense anyone else, so Thomas Hartfield had ventured out to meet her alone.

'You stopped being my *dad* when you murdered my mother.'

'That was unfortunate.' He leaned back against the bench and stretched his long legs out. He was at ease, unlike Emma, who was trying to dispel the warning screams steamrolling through her mind.

'You probably won't believe me when I tell you this, but I truly loved your mother. She meant everything to me even though she was only a human.'

'Only a human!' Emma spat. 'She was stronger than you or any of your sadistic Immortal bastards.'

'Careful. You're an Immortal too.'

'I'm a Dhampir. Half vampire and half *human*. I'm as much a part of my mum as I am a part of your sick existence.'

'Is that what you think of us? We're just trying to exist in this new world the same as everyone else.'

'You feed on innocent humans, and you're waging war on half-bloods, whom, might I add, *your* family created!'

'Well, I'm glad to see the Haven has clued you in on your family history. At least they got that right.'

'Oh, I know all about our family, Daddy dearest. I know how you and the other Immortals terrorised women for centuries and forced them to mate with you as you all raced to create the first Dhampir.'

'I never forced your mother into anything. She knew what I was, and she still loved me. That's why we married.'

'Liar!'

'It's not a lie, Emma.' He sat forward and grabbed Emma's hands. 'Watch and then tell me I'm lying.'

Emma's eyes wavered until the black of the night disappeared. The whalebone arch, Whitby Harbour, and the bench they were sitting on were replaced by a long stretch of sand and waves lapping gently on the shore. Two figures strolled hand in hand on the sand at the edge of the water. The footprints they left behind were washed away with every rush of water as it ebbed and flowed with the current.

The young woman wore a floaty dress that skimmed her ankles and got soaked as she walked. Her musical laughter filled the air as the young man scooped her up and carried her along the rest of the beach.

Her bronzed arms wrapped around him as she kissed him and giggled. It was an image of love and happiness—a picture of a summer romance that left a lasting impression.

The image flickered and changed. The same couple were outside Hartfield Manor, running across the broad expanse of lawn laughing and chasing one another. They collapsed in a heap on a picnic blanket and nestled into each other's arms.

Another shift, another picture. This time a wedding with beautiful white roses threaded through a garden pagoda. A sprinkling of guests was seated around the happy couple, and Emma saw Flora. Her hair was a pale blonde rather than the grey Emma was used to seeing. Flora was smiling at the man and woman who were exchanging rings and kissing beneath a blue sky.

The wedding scene vanished, and Emma was inside a grand room with high, ornately decorated ceilings. Wood panelling covered the walls and oil paintings were evenly spaced around the perimeter. Large leather sofas dominated the room, facing a roaring fire. Emma could almost feel the heat as the flames flickered in the grate.

The young woman was snuggled against the young man as he gently kissed the top of her head. His free hand stroked her swollen belly as they lay entwined on the sofa. The light and shadows from the fire danced across their features.

Contentment radiated from her mother's face as she placed her hand over her husband's, and together they cradled her stomach.

Thomas let go of Emma's hands, and she was back on the bench. Her head swam and her mouth was dry.

'What was that?' The visions had disorientated her.

'One of my gifts is that I'm able to show you my past.' Thomas spoke softly. 'I wanted to show you how much your mother meant to me, and that she loved me willingly.'

Emma could feel the tremors in her hands as she tried to contain her rising anger. There was no denying that the couple in the visions was in love, but true love meant cherishing one another—not murdering them.

'You killed her.' Emma said the words slowly, deliberately.

'That wasn't my intention. They took her away from me when she went into labour. By the time I got to her, she'd delivered, and then it was too late. They deceived me. They told me Charlotte would be fine, but then I learned the truth from the Deveroux family.

'The Deveroux had succeeded in creating a Dhampir first, but the host—the mother—changed over time into something inhuman. She almost killed the entire family. Only one person survived and was able to finish her before she could wipe him out too. The strength and ferocity of the child she'd carried had tainted her blood and turned her into a monster. I couldn't let your mother become that, and I knew she wouldn't want to harm her children.'

'So, murdering my mother was an act of mercy, was it? You plunged your knife into her heart before she could right your wrongs.'

Emma felt physically sick. Yes, her parents had been in love, but there was no excuse for what Thomas had done.

'James told me there was no way Charlotte would survive the transition, because she had given birth to two Dhampirs. The threat was too much.'

James. The sound of his name brought her back to the present.

'How would James know such a thing, and how do *you* know James?'

Thomas adjusted the cuff of his shirt, crossing and uncrossing his legs as he did so, and Emma realised he had spoken without thinking.

'James Deveroux was speaking from experience when he told me what would happen to your mother.'

Emma jumped to her feet and began pacing in front of the bench. *James Deveroux.* Deveroux—one of the other Immortal families. James was an Immortal, and he'd been living in the Haven under false pretences. How long had he been planning the downfall of the half-bloods? Kai had been right to be wary of him. The enemy had been right under their noses.

'I need you and Amelia with me,' Thomas said softly. 'We're family. We belong together.'

'You're not my family! You mean nothing to me; Amelia means nothing to me.'

'You don't mean that. We want you to come home, Emma.'

She stopped pacing long enough to stare at her father, sitting on the lone bench at the top of the cliff. The ocean roared around them.

Standing a little taller, Emma took a deep breath and grounded herself. Far too much information had assaulted her mind, and it would take some processing. But she knew categorically that she would never call Hartfield Manor her home while Thomas and Amelia lived there.

'Let me make this as easy as I can for you,' she said. 'The only way I would come home with you is if hell were to freeze over and probably not even then. You're a monster, and you've used my sister against me to hurt and to murder the people I care about. The only interest I have in my Immortal family is severing your heads from your bodies and watching your body parts burn before I bury them in the earth.'

'Don't be foolish, Emma. The half-bloods aren't your family. They are weak and tainted. It's fated that you'll join your sister at Hartfield Manor. It will happen even if I have to force that union. The Immortal families are returning to power, and there's nothing you can do to stop it. Join us. Come back to be with your rightful family.'

Emma shook her head and laughed. 'My rightful family! You killed the only family I had, and you've hurt my new family. I wish my mother had survived long enough to turn into the monster you claim she would have been, so she could have murdered all of you.'

'You don't know what you're talking about, girl!' Thomas's voice boomed around them, and he stood up from the bench to tower over Emma.

'Girl! Now he drops the fatherly mask.' Emma snarled and took a step back. 'You aren't my father. You were dead to me the second you murdered my mother. But you're right about one thing. I do have a destiny to fulfil, but it's not the one your family scrawled into the

Codex. No, my destiny is the one my mother left for me. I will never join you and Amelia. I refuse to unite the Immortal families, but I promise you here and now that I will be the one to end you. I will bring the Immortal families to their knees.'

She turned and ran. She became a blur on the horizon as she escaped the impending wrath of her Immortal father. Like the bomb they had uncovered in the Haven, Emma had just detonated something else—her own self-preservation powered by the black cloak that coated every inch of her soul. If the Hartfields wanted a war, then they were going to get one.

It was time to fight darkness with darkness.

12

'You're telling me James is an Immortal, your dad is alive and kicking, and you've threatened to kill them all?' Kai rubbed the back of his neck.

'Yes, that pretty much sums it up!' Emma said.

'Oh, that's bad. That's really bad,' Simran mumbled.

Emma, Kai, Dylan, and Simran were huddled in one corner of the barn discussing the unsettling discoveries Emma had made on the clifftop the previous evening.

'Why would you do that?' Kai asked.

'Why?' Emma looked at him incredulously. 'Would you prefer I joined my sister and let them turn us both into a powerful weapon against the Haven and everyone in this barn?'

'Well, no. When you put it like that, I guess threatening an evil Immortal with war was your only option,' said Kai.

'Precisely!'

'How do you know that's your father's plan?' Simran asked.

'I don't, but he seemed so desperate to get Amelia and me together. Plus, she's had plenty of opportunities to kill me, but I'm still here.'

'She was the one who turned you the night you were attacked,' Dylan said. 'Maybe that was the point. They wake your dormant Dhampir side, knowing that the Haven will swoop in and take you.

Then they hope that your Hartfield nature kicks in, and you murder us all in our beds.'

'I guess they weren't banking on my human side being so damn strong then,' Emma said with a half-hearted laugh. It wasn't funny. None of it was. They were all in danger, and she had made it ten times worse. But in her heart, or the space where it had once beat, she knew standing against the Immortal families was the right thing to do.

The barn door opened, and Dustin bustled through. His broad shoulders dominated the doorframe as he nodded at the remaining Haven inhabitants strewn around the farm building. He made his way to Emma, clutching a package in his hands.

'Hey, princess, this was delivered to the cottage for you.' He handed the parcel over.

'We told you to stay away from the cottage, Dustin!' Simran snapped at him. 'We don't want Amelia getting to you again.'

Dustin wrapped his arm around Simran's shoulder and squeezed. 'Don't you worry about me, Sim. I can look after myself.'

Simran sighed and nestled her head against his chest. She had been overly cautious and protective since Jess's death, and the rest of the group took extra time to reassure her that everyone was safe, even if it was a lie.

Emma ripped open the parcel and pulled out the wooden frame containing the photograph of her and Flora. It was the one from her nightstand back in Allendale—the only picture she had of the two of them together. This was Flora's way of telling her she was thinking of her and supporting her even from afar.

'What a lovely photo.' Dustin peered over Emma's shoulder. 'That was nice of Flora to send it to you.'

Emma was about to agree when she caught the scent on the envelope. Many months ago, she had held this frame in her bedroom and smelt an odour that she hadn't recognised as she'd looked around their broken home. But that was before she'd met Amelia. She knew the scent now, and a chill settled in her bones.

'When was this delivered?' She spun to face Dustin, thrusting the large envelope toward him.

'About an hour ago. I was checking on the cat, and the postman stopped to drop it off.'

'What is it?' Dylan asked.

'I think Flora is in danger.'

'How do you know?' Dylan studied the envelope in Emma's hand.

'Amelia's scent is all over the frame and package.'

'What do you want to do?' Dylan asked.

'I need to go home. I have to check that she's safe. Amelia has threatened her too many times.'

'We'll come with you,' Simran said.

'I can't ask you to do that,' said Emma.

'You're not asking,' Simran added. 'We're offering.'

Emma looked at her friends, and something melted inside her. Flora had told her that family wasn't always blood, and she was slowly starting to recognise that.

'Cara will be pissed if we don't tell her where we're going,' Dylan said.

The four friends glanced across the barn to where Cara and Pierce were sitting. Their heads were bent close together as they conversed.

'I think Cara has got her hands full here,' Emma said.

'I agree, but we still need to tell her what we're doing and why,' Dylan replied.

As if sensing they were talking about her, Cara stood up and walked toward them with a wry smile.

'Where are you lot going then?' Cara asked.

'It's Flora,' Emma said. 'She's in danger from Amelia, and I don't want her to get in the middle of all this again!'

So much had happened since Cara had turned up at Emma's door and offered her help. Friendships had been forged, broken, and rebuilt. Love had been won and lost. Betrayal, grief, and joy had filled their days, but Emma felt more in control of herself these days than ever before.

Perhaps embracing that darkness would not be as terrifying as she had assumed. Maybe her friends could help her stay grounded if she tried to unleash the Hartfield Dhampir gene that had everyone in such a fluster. Keeping herself isolated had made her feel safe, but did she truly understand what she was saving herself from? The darkness that swirled around her felt off, like a malevolent force waiting to be unleashed. Emma didn't want to see the repercussions if she set it—herself—free without someone to pull her back.

Emma still marvelled at the capabilities of her vampire friends. The powers they had made them unique, although they had never really tested their full abilities outside of missions. Whatever was to come meant they would all have to start honing their gifts.

'Okay.' Cara's voice broke into Emma's thoughts. 'Check on your grandmother but hurry back. Pierce is working on a way to retaliate. We need all the vampire power we can get, and you guys are the best we've got.'

Dylan puffed out his chest dramatically and winked at Cara, who rolled her eyes before walking away. Her long legs carried her with ease across the barn and back to where Pierce stood with Katie and another boy from their nest.

Emma couldn't help but feel overwhelmed upon seeing Katie again. Her guilt over Jess's death was driving her to annihilate Amelia and James—and now her father.

• • •

Emma didn't want to think too hard about what they might find at Flora's cottage.

Amelia had already taken Flora once, and there was a strong case for her to kidnap the old woman again. Still Emma had a niggling feeling in the pit of her stomach that Amelia, with Thomas's and James's help, was changing her tactics, and that was dangerous.

The cottage came into view as the streetlights flickered on along the road. Emma's old neighbours were beginning to close their curtains against the grey evening, and she briefly wondered if Paul Parker was doing okay. Not that she wanted to see him or drag him back into her crazy vampire life, but he was always going to be a link to home and a connection to her old life.

'Ready?' Kai asked as he stopped outside the front door.

The house was dark apart from Flora's bedroom light, which splashed a weak puddle of light down the front of the building.

Emma held on to the hope that she would find Flora either asleep with her meditation app running in the background or watching one of the documentaries she loved so much.

The house was exactly as she had left it when Cara had taken her to the Haven. The sideboard was still in the centre of the living room, although some of the broken ornaments had been cleared away. Emma felt a sudden surge of guilt about sending Flora back to a home that Amelia had destroyed. She should have come back with her, made sure it was safe, and helped clear up the mess. There was no way the older woman could move the sideboard on her own. What had she been thinking?

'Whoa, what happened?' Dylan stood in the doorway, surveying the carnage.

'Amelia,' Emma answered. 'This is how I found it when I got home the day Flora was taken.'

'No wonder you were so freaked out when you got to the Haven. This is a heavy-duty mess.' Simran swivelled around to take it all in. 'They already had their prize, so why did they do all this too?'

'Amelia's way of breaking me, I guess. She probably thought I'd run home to Daddy if they left me to stew in the clutter long enough.'

'But Cara swooped in and saved you,' Kai added.

'Yeah, she did. More than I realised.' It was the truth. The day Cara had turned up and had told Emma about the Haven was the day everything changed. Emma thought her life was over—literally, but the nest had showed her there were people like her out there. What was it Dustin had told her? Everyone was broken, but they were all survivors.

'I smell blood.' Dylan moved toward the staircase.

'It's Flora's.' Emma waved her hand dismissively. 'It's on the handrail, but I didn't get around to cleaning it before I left with Cara.'

Dylan shook his head. 'No, this is fresh.'

They all turned to the stairs that led up to Flora's bedroom. A pale light shone through the cracks around the door.

'Emma!' Simran moved in front of her to block her path, but Emma sidestepped her friend and made it to the staircase as Dylan reached the top step.

He turned the handle and pushed open the door. The stench of blood was much more pungent now that the door had been opened. The metallic tang swirled through the house, permeating everything in its path. Emma studied Dylan's reaction with growing panic. Something was wrong. Something was terribly wrong.

'Oh God—'

Emma barrelled past him and entered the small bedroom. The lamps were on in two corners of the room. They were balanced precariously on large stacks of books Flora kept close for when she had time to read.

The curtains were closed against the growing night, but they fluttered in the breeze where the glass didn't quite fit the window frame. Flora had been planning on fixing it for months.

To the right of the door, Flora's personal effects littered the dressing table: a hairbrush and comb, her pearl earrings, and a lip gloss she liked to save for special occasions. Emma took in all the tiny details of the room as she tried desperately to avoid looking at the bed.

The pull was too strong. Her gaze drifted across the floor and up to the worn cream tassels that edged the blanket, guarding the perimeter like tiny angels. She lifted her eyes to take in pale feet, and she ran her gaze up the legs until she saw the hem of a mint green nightgown.

The light green colour faded beneath a sea of red. Blood coated the bedclothes underneath Flora's torso. Her hands had been folded over her stomach, and they were drenched in blood too.

Flora's defiled corpse lay in the centre of a pool of blood. The head was missing. Emma recoiled in horror and dropped to her knees.

'Oh my God.' Simran covered her mouth as she entered the room.

Kai pulled a blanket from the chair in the corner of the room and laid it over Flora's body to hide the image that would be forever etched into their memories.

'Retribution,' Dylan mumbled. 'For turning away from Thomas and Amelia.'

Tears stained Emma's cheeks as she fought to keep the swirling pit of anger from overwhelming her. She had never felt pain like this. It screamed through her head, driving hot pokers into her limbs and pressing a weight too heavy to bear down on her chest.

'They can't get away with this,' Emma choked out.

'What can we do?' Kai's voice wavered. 'They've been one step ahead of us this whole time. They even pulled James out of their pocket like a bonus card in their macabre game.'

'We'll go back to the Haven and see what Cara and Pierce have come up with,' Simran suggested.

'There is no Haven.' Emma dragged herself to her feet. 'They took that away from us too. It's time we took everything from them.'

'How are we going to do that?' Dylan asked. 'They have a half-blood army, for God's sake.'

'We don't need an army.' Emma took one last look at Flora's body. 'We've got something much worse. We have a Hartfield.'

• • •

'No!' Cara pulled Emma off to the side so the entire barn wouldn't overhear them. 'There is no way I'm letting you go to Hartfield Manor alone. No. Never. Not happening.'

'I won't be alone,' Emma said. 'Kai, Dylan, and Sim will be with me, but nobody else needs to know that.'

'So instead of getting yourself killed, you're planning on getting my entire nest murdered?'

Emma flinched at Cara's words as Jess's death flooded her mind once again.

As if conscious of the harshness of her tone, Cara softened her voice. 'I'm sorry, Emma. I can't let you risk lives without a solid plan.'

'I have a solid plan. Kill my father, kill Amelia, and kill James—not necessarily in that order.'

'What they did to Flora was unthinkable.' Cara's voice was as soft as a whisper. 'I can't begin to imagine what you're going through, but running into the enemy's lair isn't an option.'

Dustin appeared out of nowhere clutching a large roll of creamy tissue paper. 'Cara, if I may, Emma might be onto something by going in alone.' He spread the paper out on the floor and crouched down over it, securing the corners with bricks and debris from the ground.

Dylan and Kai joined them as Dustin gestured to the blueprints of Hartfield Manor.

'I went back to the cottage.' He ignored the eye-rolls from everyone gathered. 'I needed to collect a few things and thought these plans might be useful. There is a way to access the main house from outside the perimeter wall. The tunnel was built centuries ago for the inhabitants to travel between the house and a storage facility two miles down the road. It's where they kept the slaves they fed on.'

Emma wrinkled her nose at the revelation and vowed to change her last name the first chance she got.

'The storage facility is a ruin now. It hasn't been used in years, but the tunnel should still be accessible.'

'Where does it open inside the house?' Kai stepped closer to inspect the plans.

'Here.' Dustin stabbed the blueprints with his finger. 'Right under the kitchen. There should be a panel in the floor, but it might have been covered up or sealed shut over the years. I can't guarantee that this will work, but it's an option.'

The friends turned to look at Cara, who was peering at the plans. She straightened her shoulders and crossed her arms over her chest.

A brightly coloured headscarf secured her Afro curls away from her face, and it somehow made her look younger.

'I think we have the makings of a mission,' Cara said with a wink.

'Yes!' Dylan punched the air. 'It's just like the good old days!'

Changing to business mode, Cara called the bedraggled remains of the Haven to order and took centre stage.

'We've been licking our wounds long enough,' Cara said. 'The Hartfields and James have taken our home and our family, but we may have a way to fight back.'

A rousing cheer went up as the vampires leaned in to hear more. Their interest was piqued by the promise of vengeance.

Cara invited Emma to join her. 'Do you want to add anything?'

Emma stepped forward, recalling the night Cara had let her take point on the mission over the moors. The memory stirred something inside her and enhanced the plan that was beginning to form in her mind.

'My family is the face of true evil.' Her voice was loud and strong. 'They have terrorised humans and half-bloods for centuries, but I believe it's time their rule came to an end.'

More cheers as the vampires warmed to the theme.

'Kai, Dylan, and I will infiltrate Hartfield Manor through a hidden passage. Once inside we'll draw the Immortal family out. We can't take on their army while fighting the Immortals, so we'll need your help. I need you to go out and recruit the rogue half-bloods, and any other independent nests you can find. I want you to coordinate with Simran and bring them back to Whitby Abbey—to our new Haven—to fight back against the monsters who took everything from us.'

Everyone was on their feet, clapping and cheering as Emma moved back to stand with her friends.

'Didn't know you had it in you, Em.' Dylan winked. 'You make one badass vampire!'

Emma chuckled but was relieved that her plan to recruit the rogue vampires had worked. It was a gamble. Some nest leaders like Pierce had adhered strictly to the Haven's laws, but others like Cara had been more lenient. Joey was proof of that, and Emma hoped that he and others like him would rally to their cause.

'Clever move,' Cara said. 'Looks like we have our plan. When do you want to attack?'

'If we can rally the half-bloods and get them here before sunset tomorrow, we will move on Hartfield Manor at dawn. Hopefully, my family won't expect an attack in the day, and it will give us another advantage.'

'We'll need a signal so the rest of us know when to attack the manor once you're inside,' said Cara.

'I can handle that,' Simran said as she strolled over on the arm of a tall, muscular vampire with a shock of black hair. 'This is Zain. He was a bit of a pyrotechnician in his human life, so I figured his special skills might come in handy.'

'And I'm sure you were able to use your persuasive powers to get him to agree to your plans. Isn't that right, Sim?' Dylan added with a chuckle.

Her friends teased one another and hatched their plans to take down an Immortal family as Emma's thoughts moved to killing her father and sister. The idea both excited and terrified her. She knew what they were capable of. She couldn't deny that the earth would be a better place without them in it, but a part of her, buried deep inside, still craved that sense of belonging. James had given her a glimpse of what it was like to feel loved even if it had been an illusion.

Now she was faced with the reality of tearing her family to pieces to be free of their pull, free of the darkness.

Before she could set herself free, though, she needed to tap into the side of her she had fought against all her life. The abyss that had opened in her soul upon finding Flora's body was filling with pure rage. Flora had told her to fight darkness with darkness, and now she understood what that meant.

To take down an Immortal, she had to let the darkness swallow her whole and use it to destroy her enemies.

She needed to become the Dhampir she was born to be.

13

Half-bloods swarmed into the barn from far and wide. It appeared to be Cara's influence that brought many of the rogue vampires back. Joey was one of the first to arrive after hearing Cara was now running the show.

Emma felt a huge sense of pride in her saviour and had faith that Cara would lead them all into a new age.

'Today is the day then,' Simran said as she sharpened a wooden stake with her penknife. 'Are you nervous?'

Emma glanced at her friend, the girl with the power to get anything she wanted with a few simple words.

'Not at all,' Emma replied. 'We're all stronger than we realise. We need to believe in ourselves.'

'What do you mean?'

'Flora told me I needed to fight darkness with darkness. I didn't understand what she meant until I was staring at her corpse. Amelia is pure evil because she doesn't know any different. I've known love, friendship, and family. That's my superpower.'

'What are you planning to do? Cuddle her to death?'

Emma chuckled. 'Not quite. She might be my twin, but she's still a murderer. My darkness is her darkness, and I need to find a way to let that work in my favour. All of us need to use our gifts tonight, but I think your gift might give us the advantage.'

'What do you mean?'

'I have an idea.' Emma set down the blueprints she had been studying and took Simran's hands in her own. 'There's a way we can get Amelia's half-blood army to join us without anyone else dying.'

'How?' Simran leaned in, awaiting Emma's revelation.

'You.'

'Me!' Simran sat back, and a wrinkle crossed her otherwise flawless brow. 'How can I get an entire army to desert?'

'You tell them to. Use your siren power. Tell them they're fighting on the wrong side, and that joining us is the right thing to do. It'll give us the numbers to relaunch the Haven, and it will be a huge blow to Amelia's plans.'

Simran shook her head. 'I can't. I've only ever used my gift on small groups or one person at a time. Never on a room of over one hundred vampires.'

'Practise on us. Stand up and ask everyone in this barn to do something.'

With a gentle nudge from Emma, Simran stood and moved to the centre of the room and called for everyone's attention.

'Sorry to interrupt.' Simran glanced back at Emma, who nodded her encouragement. 'Can you all stand on one leg for a minute?'

The vampires looked around at one another, some with puzzled expressions and some with smirks, but nobody stood on one leg.

'Try again,' Emma urged, 'but mean it this time.'

Simran squared her shoulders and tried again. 'I need you all to stand on one leg for one minute.'

There was a pause, but people started to balance on one leg. Some people giggled as they did it, but before long all the inhabitants of the barn had done as Simran asked.

The shock on her beautiful face made Emma laugh, but this small win was one step closer to the downfall of the Immortal family.

'How did you do that?' Dylan asked after the minute had lapsed and everyone had gone back to their tasks in a bewildered fashion. 'I've only ever seen you use your gift on one or two people.'

'It was Emma's idea. She thinks I can turn Amelia's army into our allies.'

'That's genius,' Kai said as he joined the group of friends. 'Will it work?'

'Did you stand on one leg?' Simran crossed her arms over her chest and raised a disapproving eyebrow at him.

'Yes, I did.' Kai laughed. 'Point taken. This is a game changer. It will make all the difference if we can get inside Hartfield Manor without the risk of an army on our tail.'

'We'll still have our rogue army in case anything goes wrong,' Simran said, reminding everyone of the backup plan should her manipulation fail.

'It frees the rest of us up to take on Thomas, Amelia, and James,' Emma said.

'Oh, is that all?' Dylan said with a nervous laugh.

'We can do this,' Emma said. 'If we work together, we'll have the strength to beat them all and end this forever.'

'You seem keen to kill your family.' The voice came from behind the group, and as they turned, Joey stepped into view.

'I don't see the Hartfields as my family.' Emma looked at her friends. 'I've got all the family I need right here.'

'Good to hear,' Joey said. 'Let's hope that stays true today.'

'What's that supposed to mean?' Emma snapped, annoyed that Joey was questioning her loyalties.

'The pull of an Immortal soul is strong. Are you sure you're stronger?' Joey asked.

'I feel nothing for my father or my sister. They're the enemy. I would never—' Emma knew Joey was only voicing the same grumbling thoughts she had been battling all day. Was she strong enough to resist? Would she be strong enough to kill her own flesh and blood? Could she kill James when the time came?

'Emma is one of us,' Dylan said. 'She'll do what's right.'

'I hope you're right,' Joey said with a small smile before wandering off to speak with another group of grubby-looking rogues who had joined the quest.

'Don't listen to him,' Kai said. 'We know it's going to be tough today, but we all believe in you.'

'Thanks, Kai. I appreciate that.'

Emma resumed looking at the plans, but they blurred beneath the film of tears that coated her eyes. She refused to let the tears fall. Nothing Joey or any of the vampires could say to her was any worse than what she was thinking herself.

At her dark core, she was a Hartfield.

She shook her head as she tried to dislodge the murderous thoughts she harboured for her family. Now wasn't the time to fall apart. She had to channel that dark energy until it was needed. She was a Dhampir, not an Immortal. She was special, and today she was going to show everyone exactly how special.

· · ·

Hartfield Manor stood silhouetted against the cloudy grey sky as Emma, Kai, and Dylan left Simran, Cara, Joey, and a handful of vampires at the broken wall.

'We'll give you half an hour to get through the tunnel and into the kitchen before we scale the wall and break into the outbuildings.' Cara set a timer on her phone and synchronised it with Kai's.

'The half-blood army is split between the two buildings,' Emma told Simran. 'You'll need to work your siren magic quickly before moving to the next building.'

'I know what I have to do.' Simran pulled Emma into a tight embrace. 'When we're clear you'll hear all about it!'

Emma chuckled as Simran nodded at Zain, who was hauling a bag of explosives behind him.

'Be careful,' Emma said.

Leaving Sim behind pulled at Emma's emotions more than she'd thought possible. Since Jess's murder, Simran had been more withdrawn and vulnerable. The yin to her yang was missing, and it seemed to have thrown her off course. Emma recognised it because she too felt adrift. They had all moved on the best they could, each of them rallying around this new cause to rebuild the Haven, unite the vampires, and beat the evil threat that hung over them. But they still held on to that pain, loss, and grief. Cara had raised her nest to appreciate and honour their human side, but Emma was starting to wonder if that was a wise strategy.

Ahead loomed the derelict storage building Dustin had told them about. The walls were crumbling, and there was a gaping hole where the roof had caved in years before and never been repaired.

To the innocent eye, it was just another abandoned farm building littering the countryside, but to Emma and her party, it was their way into Hartfield Manor.

'Ready?' Kai asked.

Emma and Dylan followed Kai inside.

Thick overgrowth had invaded the space. Heavy vines and weeds wound through the cracks in the floor and walls, and a blanket of mud and moss covered the floor. According to Dustin, the entrance to the tunnel was beneath a trapdoor in the eastern corner of the building.

Sure enough, Kai's boot connected with the unmistakable rattle of an iron railing, and after clearing the debris, they uncovered the entrance. The gate was rusted shut, and it took all three of them to pry it open with rocks and wooden planks they salvaged from the ground.

It groaned and creaked, eventually swinging open to reveal a dark passageway in the ground. It ran off to the left in the direction of Hartfield Manor.

'Want me to check it out?' Dylan asked with a twinkle in his eye. He thrived in these situations. He loved the missions he was sent on and excelled at finding what was lost.

'Yeah, go ahead,' Kai said, 'but be careful.'

Dylan jumped into the hole and disappeared down the tunnel, leaving Kai and Emma to follow at a steady vampire pace.

By the time they caught up with their friend, he had fought his way through an abundance of spiderwebs and an assortment of neglected crates to uncover a set of concrete stairs leading up to another trapdoor. The door should open in the heart of the manor if Dustin's blueprints were correct.

Kai checked the timer he had set on his phone. 'Two minutes till Simran will be over the wall and infiltrating the outbuildings.'

They waited patiently. If this was a success, the half-bloods would be free of the shadow of war cast by the Immortal families, and Emma would be free of her darkness.

'Let's go!' Kai made his way up the staircase toward the wooden barrier.

Dylan and Emma joined Kai as they pushed against the door. It shifted slightly, and Emma could see through the sliver of space.

'It's the kitchen,' she said. 'I can see the units and the main door from here. It looks empty.'

They heaved against the wood until a loud crack filled the air. The door split in two under the force of their vampire strength. Emma climbed out of the stairway and into the kitchen with her stake and sword at the ready.

The house was silent.

'They won't be asleep for long once Sim's explosives go off,' Kai whispered. 'Do you know where Amelia and your father are?'

'I think I can track them,' Emma said.

The trio navigated their way around the steel units toward the main kitchen door and into a large living space beyond. The entrance hall was visible through the opening at the far side of the room. The wooden floors gleamed, and the high ceilings were ornately decorated. Wood panelling covered the walls, with oil paintings hanging evenly around its perimeter.

Emma stopped short. She recognised this room from Thomas's vision. She took in her surroundings, and her gaze settled on the large leather sofas in front of the open fire. There were no flames today, but the image of her parents nestled into each other's arms dominated her memory. Her mother had been here in this very room, carrying her twin girls. She'd believed their lives would be good, and the love she'd had for Thomas had been clear in the way she'd cradled him and her swollen stomach.

'I don't know if I can do this,' she muttered suddenly as she ran her hand along the old leather sofa.

'What? You can't back out now,' Kai hissed. 'You'll get us all killed.'

Emma lifted her face to look at her friends. They had followed her into the lion's den willingly. Was she seriously going to feed them to the Hartfield monsters?

A loud explosion filled the air, rattling the windows of the old house. There was no turning back now.

Slow, methodical clapping echoed around the room as Thomas walked into view. Two guards flanked him, but there was no sign of Amelia or James.

'I'm impressed,' Thomas said. 'Storming the castle in the daylight and blowing up my outbuildings is a bold move. Does my daughter finally understand her destiny?'

Emma bristled. She felt only loathing for the man who now blocked their escape route, but she also battled against her conflicting feelings of loyalty to her mother.

'I don't have a destiny.' Emma removed her hand from the sofa and placed it on the handle of the sword Dustin had given her.

'You have family.' Thomas stretched his arms wide. 'Isn't family a form of destiny?'

'No! You and Amelia destroyed my true family, and you took away the only person I had in the world.'

'Flora wasn't family. She was a mere complication—someone your mother chose to trust over her husband. If Charlotte had listened to me instead of that old crone, maybe she would still be alive today.'

'That's a lie! You told me you had to kill my mother before she turned on you and us.'

'Ah, yes. Perhaps I bent the truth slightly.' He waved his arm around as if lying was something that came naturally to him. 'You see, a Dhampir has great power but not enough to give the Immortal family the power it needs. Your dear friend James is evidence of this phenomenon as he too is a Dhampir.'

Emma felt like she'd had the wind knocked out of her. James was a Dhampir.

'It appears that male Dhampirs are only good for their amplified vampire talents. They don't have what it takes to restore the Immortal families to glory.'

Thomas began to walk around the room as his two guards inched forward. Dylan and Kai drew their swords and flanked Emma.

'Your brave friends can't help you, my girl. Unless they stand down, I will be forced to kill them both and make you watch.'

Emma shook her head, and the boys lowered their swords.

'How did James's inadequacies lead to the death of my mother?'

Thomas chuckled and came to a stop in front of the empty fireplace. 'It was written in the Codex that only a female Dhampir could restore our families, so when your mother and I were told she was having you, we were delighted. But at a later scan, we discovered a second heartbeat.'

'Amelia!'

'Indeed. Your mother was having twins. She was excited about having two girls, but the Codex told another story.'

Emma fought with her memories as she recalled reading the Codex with Dustin.

'The sisters will prevail,' she mumbled.

A sudden realisation hit Emma, and she felt a lightness about her that she had not experienced for a very long time.

'It didn't mean we could *restore* the Immortal families,' she said with an understanding smile. 'It meant that we were the only ones who could destroy you.'

Using the revelation as a distraction, Dylan launched himself at the first guard and staked him before he had time to draw his weapon.

Kai moved on the second, turning him to red mist before he could register what was happening.

Thomas stalked toward the entrance hall, but Emma blocked his path.

'Not yet, Daddy. We haven't finished our chat.'

She rested the point of her sword on his throat and watched the tiny pinprick of blood bubble up against the blade where she pressed it against his skin.

'Flora took my mother from you when it was time to give birth, didn't she?'

'Yes. Charlotte learned of the Dhampir legend to destroy the Immortal line—a curse handed down by the tribes that created us. She fled to have you in secret.'

'But you found them.' She pressed the sword tighter and delighted in seeing Thomas wince. 'You were going to murder all of us that night.'

'It's not what I wanted!' Thomas threw his hands in the air despite the pinch of the blade at his throat. 'I loved your mother, and I would have loved you. The choice was taken away from me.'

'So, you murdered Flora to get your revenge.'

'That was Amelia's doing. Your sister isn't as empathetic as you are. She believed you would come back to us if you had no one else.'

'Murder Flora, destroy the Haven, and then what, I'll skip happily up the front drive and rush into your open arms?'

'Your sister doesn't have your qualities, Emma. She only did what she thought was right, however misguided.'

Emma lowered the blade slightly as Kai and Dylan approached.

'We'll clear the house and search for Amelia and James,' Kai said. 'Cara should be joining us soon.' He glanced up at Thomas as he said it.

Thomas smiled and continued to lean against the doorjamb. 'You found a way to unite the half-bloods.' It was a statement rather than a question.

'We have,' Dylan answered him anyway.

'I'm even more impressed,' Thomas said with a slight hitch to his voice.

Emma nodded at her friends as they left but spun on her father when they were out of range.

'You've lost, and yet you sound perfectly calm. Are you so secure in your Immortal status that you think you'll survive this?'

Thomas studied her with a gleam in his eye.

'You won't kill me. Not when you crave answers to your many questions.'

'There's nothing you can say that would interest me.'

'I doubt that.' He examined his fingernails. 'The day you were born, I intended to kill only one of you. Dhampir twins have the power to destroy us all, but a single Dhampir can be nurtured in the ways of our family.'

Emma reeled at the revelation. Their father was prepared to do anything in his quest for power. Even sacrificing one of his children.

'James Deveroux told me the truth about Charlotte planning to leave me. Your mother had grown concerned about the safety of her babies and had turned to him for help. He used his unique power to see inside her mind, and he was able to connect to you and Amelia. He sensed great darkness and told her of his worries.'

Part of Emma didn't want to listen as she tried to calm the inner turmoil that swirled through her. The other part of her wondered if that darkness *had* been with them in the womb. If so, it was no wonder she felt so consumed by it.

'She thought she was having evil twins,' Emma said softly.

'No, James told her that one of the babies was cloaked in darkness, but the other one was fighting back. He told her about the Codex and the legend, but she refused to believe her girls were capable of destroying the Immortal families.'

'She ran away because she knew you would have to kill one of her babies.'

'Yes.' He dropped his hands to his sides.

'But when you got to the hospital, she'd already given birth. Why the hell did you still kill her?'

Tears filled his eyes, and Emma took a step backwards, shocked at the vulnerability of this powerful Immortal vampire.

'When I saw your mother in the hospital bed, I was overcome with rage. She took my babies and left, choosing a human life over the one I could give her. I never intended to kill her. I only ever wanted her with me, here at Hartfield Manor.' He looked around the room as if remembering all the times they had spent together under the ornate ceiling.

'You killed her because of who you are—a vampire.'

'My instincts overtook everything else, and I'd struck before I realised what I was doing. I've been a vampire for centuries, Emma. It's a curse that permeates every part of who you are.'

Emma laughed. 'You're saying that I should forgive you because murder is in your nature?'

'I don't want your forgiveness. I don't deserve it, but I do need your help. That's why I established James within the Haven, so he would be able to protect you if your Dhampir curse was ever activated. I knew the Haven would find you eventually.'

'James has been with the Haven for centuries, and I've only been alive for seventeen years.'

'I hope that one day you'll understand how powerful an Immortal vampire can be. It was a simple manipulation on my part to make the council leaders believe James had always been one of them. A mind warp if you like. Once I created the illusion of James being on the council, they did the rest by sharing the Codex with him, keeping him updated about your life and death, and including him in their sessions, so he was there to meet you when you got there.'

Emma thought back to her initial meeting with the Haven council, and how they were all seated in a semicircle. James had sat off to the side, away from the rest of the established leaders. Her mind flicked to the recreation hall when he had first spoken to her, and the way he moved through the crowds without anyone talking to him or looking at him.

Had her entire life been mapped out and controlled from afar?

'You were safe as a human. None of us could find you. Flora did her job well in keeping you safe, but your sister stumbled across your mother's diaries. When she learned about you, she became obsessed.'

'She sent a vampire to murder me, and then she activated my Dhampir side. Her obsession destroyed my life and hurt my family and friends. Normal people send an email!'

Emma lowered her sword as they stood talking in the doorway of the living room that held so many memories of her mother and father. Behind them was the entrance hall of the manor, where hundreds of half-bloods were about to pour inside and take control of her ancestral home.

'I'm sorry, Emma. When Amelia told me you had awoken, I was overcome with a desire to reunite my family, but I realise that was a foolish quest. I hoped I would be able to disprove the legend of the Codex and bring my girls together, but there's too much darkness.'

Emma laughed. The darkness had pooled around her, flowing through her veins and forcing her into self-isolation. She had feared harming those around her, and now her Immortal family had decided she was too dark even for them.

'Are you saying I'm too evil to be part of your evil family?'

Thomas shook his head. 'No, you misunderstand me. You're not evil, Emma. Amelia is the one who harbours pure darkness in her soul. You fought against her even before your mother brought you into the world. You are the light, the power of the Immortal family, and the Dhampir capable of restoring the Hartfield name to glory. Together, you and your sister would destroy us, but with her gone, your strength could reinstate honour to our name.'

'What are you saying?'

'Amelia was the one I meant to kill at the hospital that night, but after I killed your mother and Flora snatched you away, I was left with nothing. I couldn't kill her. I brought her home and hoped James's visions were wrong.'

Emma was speechless. Thomas was telling her that she was good, pure—the one with the power to save the family. It went against everything she had believed her entire life.

'I can't restore the Immortal families,' she said finally. 'I won't bring about more death and destruction.'

'That's not what any of us want, Emma. The Immortal families need help to find their way in the new world. We have lived without female guidance for too long. The curse left us feral and fighting amongst ourselves. I've lived so many lifetimes, and the only one that mattered was the one I spent with your mother. Restoring the Immortal families doesn't mean returning to the old ways. It means finding a new path.'

She hardly believed what Thomas was saying, yet the gaping hole in her chest began to fill with love and hope.

Shouts from upstairs tore her attention away, and she turned from Thomas to run into the centre of the entrance hall. Kai was limping down the grand staircase as blood poured from a gash in his arm.

'Amelia!' Kai pointed back up the stairs.

The front door burst open, and Cara rushed through followed by Simran and the half-blood army. Emma glanced over to where she had left Thomas, half expecting him to have run. Instead, he stood firm in the doorway, smiling at her with pride.

Dylan's scream filled the air as Amelia threw him over the railing, and he tumbled down the staircase, landing heavily at Emma's feet.

'She's coming,' Dylan said, moaning.

Two words that filled Emma with dread.

For all his faults, Thomas had kept Amelia alive because of the love he had for their mother, but that meant the task of killing her now fell to Emma.

She helped Dylan to his feet and motioned for Simran to help Kai.

'What's the plan?' Cara asked as she assessed the layout of the room and checked on her team's injuries.

'We can't let Amelia get away,' Emma said.

'What about him?' Cara gestured at Thomas, who remained in the doorway.

Emma knew she should be telling Cara to destroy the man—that he was a monster the world could do without—but something tugged at her. A sense of loyalty. Perhaps Joey was right, after all. Maybe she wasn't strong enough to turn away from the pull of her Immortal family.

She was about to tell Cara her father needed to be imprisoned until a new council could decide what to do with him when Amelia appeared at the top of the stairs.

'How touching,' Amelia said. 'My dear sister has reunited with our father, and the first thing he did was tell you to kill me.'

'You murdered Flora,' Emma hissed, 'and you murdered our friends. You deserve to die.'

Amelia laughed. The hollow sound punctured the air. She jumped over the railing, landing squarely in front of Emma with a sword in one hand and a wooden stake in the other.

'If you want to kill me, here I am.'

Amelia didn't wait for Emma to move; instead, she flung the stake at Cara. The action unfolded as if in slow motion as the weapon sailed toward its mark. At the last second, Joey jumped in front of Cara, and the wooden stake embedded into his chest.

'No!' Cara screamed as Joey convulsed before exploding into red mist, coating everyone in the vicinity. Cara's bright eyes hardened as she turned toward Amelia. She ran at the vampire with a painful cry that hit Emma hard in the gut.

Amelia spun away from the attack with ease and cut down two more of the half-bloods as they rallied behind Cara's advance.

Emma launched herself at her sister, swinging her blade in a wide arc and catching Amelia on the upper arm. The girl smiled in the inhuman way only she was capable of.

'You cut me.' Amelia stopped mid-stride. 'There's hope for you yet.'

It felt good to cause Amelia pain, however small it might be, but Emma was fully aware of her severe lack of combat training. Kai and Simran had done their best to show her the basics, but as she pulled her sword back, she knew her limited skills were no match for her sister.

Amelia retaliated and came at Emma with strike after strike. Emma dodged, rolled, and deflected her attacks with steely determination.

In her peripheral vision, Emma noticed the dazed expressions of Amelia's half-bloods as they somehow awoke from Simran's siren call. Cara, Kai, and Dylan hurled themselves into the fight—half-blood against half-blood.

Despite the battle raging around them, Amelia and Emma circled one another as if cut off from the world by an invisible force. Sisters united in darkness. A sneer stretched across Amelia's face.

The pain she inflicted brought her a sick satisfaction. If a half-blood ventured too close, she would cut them down. Her joy and thirst for a fight were palpable.

Emma's arm grew heavy as she blocked the relentless attacks. Her clothes were littered with cuts where Amelia had sliced at her. Her blood pooled on her skin, staining the fabric.

'I will end you.' Amelia grabbed a handful of Emma's shirt and pulled her close. 'There is no need for a weak Dhampir in this world.'

Flora's sweet voice drifted into Emma's memory as she stared into the cold, black eyes of her twin. *'Maybe it's time you embraced that part of yourself and fought darkness with darkness.'*

Could that be the answer? Did Emma need to become Amelia to beat her? Although the thoughts were fleeting, Emma couldn't deny the power behind them. Letting the darkness that had followed her since childhood into her soul might turn her into the abomination standing before her. Or it could set her free.

Emma struck forward, smashing her forehead into Amelia's nose. She heard the crunch and felt the spray of blood as her sister let go of her shirt and stumbled backwards.

'You bitch!'

It was Emma's turn to sneer as she reached out with her mind to find the edge of the shadows that cloaked her. She tugged on something potent, but it snapped back into place just as quickly. Was that her Dhampir power?

Amelia recovered and launched at Emma with a flurry of punches to her head. She blocked the strikes as best she could, but her sister was a cold-blooded vampire with a tenacious craving for pain and destruction. A punch to the gut floored Emma, and she dropped to her knees, coughing. The room spun, but she couldn't give in. It would be too easy to curl up on the ground and admit defeat despite the roaring desire to win flooding through her veins.

The darkness wasn't going to help her now. She knew it was there, lurking in her subconscious, but with nobody to guide her, she didn't know how to access it.

Flora's voice reached her once again. *'You're as much human as you are vampire. You're special.'*

Special. Everyone kept calling her that, but Emma couldn't accept it. Yes, she was a Dhampir rather than a half-blood, but there was nothing special about it. Her Dhampir status couldn't even save her life when she needed it.

'When I'm done with you, I'm going to peel the flesh off your little half-blood friends over there and finish this.' Amelia grabbed a handful of Emma's hair as Emma kneeled on the floor.

Emma glanced to her left at Kai and Dylan fighting back-to-back. Their faces were dirty and bloody. She could see Cara hacking down the swarm of Amelia's army, and Simran was coated in the red mist that seemed to hover like a cloud over everyone. Her friends fought on, their strength and determination to win this fight driving them forward.

It wasn't darkness that rushed through Emma's body at the thought of anyone harming them, it was love and light. She curled her fingers around the hilt of the sword at her feet and braced against the floor. Nobody was going to hurt her friends—her family.

The searing pain in her scalp as Amelia twisted her hair didn't deter Emma. She jumped to her feet, shoving Amelia in the chest and giving herself some breathing room. Emma immediately brought her sword up but wasn't quick enough to make contact. Instead, she found herself turned around with a dagger at her throat.

'Too slow,' Amelia said in Emma's ear.

A primal sound rumbled up from Emma's throat as she looked out across the entrance hall at her friends. Something stirred deep within her; whether it was the darkness or something else, she didn't know. The flood of emotion was enough to give Emma the kick she needed.

Emma struck Amelia on the side of the head with the butt of her sword. Amelia released her grip on the dagger and landed heavily on the floor. The girl rallied, cursing and scrambling for her own weapon, but Emma saw her chance. Using her forward momentum, Emma brought her sword down hard.

It clashed with another blade thrust out to defend Amelia as she lay sprawled on the floor. Emma whirled around to see James standing in front of her. His weapon was the only reason Amelia still lived.

'I'm sorry, Emma. I can't let you kill her.'

The roar filling Emma's mind threatened to unhinge her. Why was he doing this? What hold did Thomas and Amelia have over James Deveroux that he would participate in their war?

'Move.' Emma's voice was as hard as stone. 'Or I'll kill you first.'

'You won't kill me,' he whispered. 'You love me.'

Emma took a step back. Her sword quivered in her hand. She stared at James and then at her sister, who was slowly lifting herself from the floor.

'I don't love you.' She spat. 'Nobody can love someone who betrays the people who care about them and fights with the enemy.'

Amelia scooped her sword from the ground and lifted the blade toward Emma. 'Don't worry, James,' Amelia crooned, cocking her head to the side and eyeing Emma up and down like a predator sizing up its prey. 'She could never love you like I do.'

Emma recoiled as if she had received another physical punch to the gut. Was James intimate with Amelia too?

A bolt of rage shot through Emma's body, and she roared, swinging her sword toward them. They disappeared from her sight. James vanished into the dark corridor behind him, and Amelia threw herself back into the fight.

As Amelia danced around the entrance hall slashing vampires, Emma realised too late that she was heading for Thomas. She couldn't let her take their father away.

'Amelia, stop!'

Emma's sister came to a halt beside Thomas. Her face was covered in blood, making her look more deranged than ever.

'There's nowhere for you to run,' Emma said. 'We will get control of your half-blood army and Hartfield Manor. It's over.'

Amelia snarled at her. 'You're so right, Emma. It is over.' With a wicked gleam in her eye, she spun her sword and beheaded Thomas before disappearing through the kitchen.

14

The fire roared in the grate, but not even the heat from the flames warmed the chill running through Emma's veins.

Ever since James had disappeared and Amelia had murdered their father, Emma had been unable to sleep. Night after night, she curled up on the grand leather sofa in the living room with the ornate ceilings and oil paintings, staring into the fire.

She somehow felt closer to her parents here. Knowing they had once sat in the same spot she now occupied gave her a small amount of comfort.

Cara had overseen the burning of Thomas's body, and his ashes now resided in the grey urn nestled in Emma's lap. When night fell, she would take the urn to St Mary's Churchyard behind Whitby Abbey and bury him in the consecrated ground.

'Hey, princess.' Dustin poked his head around the door and smiled. 'Need some company?'

Emma nodded. She feared that if she tried to speak, it would come out as a squeak or a sob.

'Everyone has gone back to the barn to regroup. Cara doesn't think it's a good idea to return to the bunker while Amelia is still at large. I guess I'll never get back to my cottage at this rate.'

Emma slipped her hand into his and squeezed. 'I'm so sorry, Dustin. If I hadn't come into your life, you'd still have your lovely home. Jess and Joey would still be alive and so would Henric and the others.'

'You can't think like that. Your fate was mapped out before you were born, but your destiny hasn't been fulfilled yet.'

'My destiny? My father told me I had the power to create a new future, but all I've managed to do is get him killed, let my psycho sister escape, and cause pain and heartache for everyone I've met.'

'That's not true. You inspired people to work together. You united the Haven half-bloods and the rogues and helped start rebuilding the Haven when everyone thought it was hopeless.'

'How have we rebuilt the Haven? We live in a draughty barn behind Whitby Abbey in constant fear that Amelia and James will murder us in our sleep.'

Emma sat up straight and placed her father's urn on the coffee table. An idea bubbled in the back of her mind. It would set them all on a new path—just as her father had predicted. 'I know what to do.' She glanced at Dustin.

She swept her arms out to the side, jumping up from the sofa as she did so. 'This can be the new Haven. Hartfield Manor is my ancestral home. With Thomas gone, it would pass to his family, and that's me. We can rebuild the Haven here.'

Dustin let out a long, low whistle.

'It's a fabulous idea, princess. There's certainly plenty of room for everyone. We could even bring in the rogues from the area. But if this place belongs to Thomas's children, then it also belongs to Amelia.'

Emma bristled at the mention of her sister.

'She lost any right to this place when she murdered our father. Don't you worry, Dustin. I'll find her. I promise you that.'

• • •

Emma's idea to use Hartfield Manor as the new base for the Haven was met with a rousing cheer when she and Dustin broached it the next evening.

It didn't take long to rally the united vampires and move them to the manor. With the demise of Amelia's rule, her vampire army gave in and joined the new Haven organisation. Simran's manipulation may not have lasted in battle, but she no longer needed to influence them. Cara and Pierce took charge, and nobody questioned their authority.

'This was a fine plan, Emma,' Cara said as she directed each nest to their new rooms. 'It gives us a base to start over and build a new reputation for the Haven. Henric's outdated policy of banishing vampires is over. Together we're going to create something special.'

Emma loved seeing the sparkle return to Cara's eyes. Since Joey had heroically sacrificed himself for her, she had been withdrawn, but now she had a cause to rally around. It had been a unanimous decision to put Cara and Pierce in charge, and Emma knew the vampires had chosen well.

'I've allocated your father's rooms to you,' Cara added. 'It seemed like the right thing to do. You'll have Sim in there with you though, so don't thank me yet!'

Emma giggled. 'That's perfect.'

Dylan strode over to where they were standing and slid his arm around Emma's shoulders.

'I'm loving Hartfield Manor.' He grinned lopsidedly. 'I take back everything I said about it being the evilest building in the county.'

Emma laughed and slapped his arm away. 'It's not an evil building, but it did house evil inhabitants.'

'You're right about that.' Kai's face was a picture of agitation. 'I think there's something you should see.'

Cara handed the rooming list over to another vampire and followed Kai, Dylan, and Emma up the staircase. Simran was waiting for them halfway down the corridor, biting at her bottom lip as she watched them approach.

'What is it?' Emma asked. The familiar sliver of ice wound its way up her spine.

'It's Amelia's bedroom.' Simran pushed the door open.

The five of them walked into the room. Every wall was covered in photographs, blueprints, maps, and scribbled sheets of paper. A single bed occupied the centre of the room, but apart from that, there were no other pieces of furniture. No desk or drawers, no wardrobe, no personal effects, no clothes. It resembled a prison cell rather than a bedroom.

On the smaller wall where the window looked out over the front drive, there was a series of black-and-white photographs.

'Who are these people?' Simran asked.

Emma trailed her fingers over the images.

'They're my parents. That's my mother, and that's Thomas.'

'He doesn't look like he did the other day,' Simran said. 'He seems…happy.'

A solitary tear trailed down Emma's cheek as she gazed at the only photographs she had ever seen of her mum and dad together. Simran was right; they seemed blissfully happy.

'Is that you?' Dylan broke into Emma's thoughts, and she wandered over to where he stood looking at a cluster of colour photographs.

'Yes, but that was taken when I was about fifteen.' Emma snatched the image from the wall. It showed a younger Emma walking home from school, clutching her bag to her side and hurrying along with her head down. In the background, Paul Parker and his friends were sitting on a bench, ignoring the loner who kept to herself.

'It looks like Amelia was watching you long before she attacked,' Kai said, 'and after.' He pointed at another picture of Emma crouched over a boy on the ground while two other boys stood to the side.

'That was a few days after Amelia turned me. I lost it with some bullies. When I went home after this, Flora was missing.'

'She documented your life—watched for patterns, weaknesses, and strengths. She knew what she was doing,' Kai said.

'Do you think Thomas was in on it?' Simran asked.

Emma had wondered the same thing. He'd said he had wanted her to remain human and safe. That he was only interested in getting her back once she was a Dhampir. Had he instructed Amelia to find her, or had her sister acted alone?

'I'm not sure. Part of me wants to believe that everything he told me and showed me in his visions was the truth, but I'm not so foolish to discount it being a ploy to get me to join the family.'

'We need to collect all of this and go through each piece carefully,' Cara said. 'It might give us some hints to her whereabouts. If we can find her first, it'll help us keep everyone at the Haven safe. We don't even know if James is with her, so any clues that will help us piece it all together are vital.'

The friends began taking the photographs and maps off the walls and created piles on the bed.

It felt strange to Emma that everything on these walls was connected to her in some way. Amelia had heard Thomas confess that he'd planned to kill her in the hospital the day they were born. That had to be the catalyst that pushed her to murder him. He had been in Amelia's life from the beginning. Emma thought that might have meant something to Amelia, but instead she had chosen to end his life. Nothing and nobody mattered to her sister.

'Let's clear the entire room.' Cara stood back to look at the space. 'I don't want anyone sleeping in here. We'll turn it into an operations room or something.'

'I like that idea.' Dylan grabbed one end of the single wooden bedframe and picked it up with ease.

'Wait!' Kai crouched down. 'There's something underneath.'

He pulled a large glass container filled with a thick, murky liquid into view. Emma felt uneasy as she surveyed the object.

'Maybe it's another bomb?' Simran took a small step backwards.

Kai handled it with some trepidation and tipped it to the side. His jaw clenched, and he flinched away from the jar, setting it down on the floor.

'What? Kai, what is it?' Emma asked.

'I'm so sorry, Emma. I don't think you should see this.'

Telling her not to do something merely made her want to do it even more. She dropped to her knees by Kai's side and studied the jar.

As the liquid sloshed around, a bloated face bumped against the side of the glass. Flora's dead eyes gazed out at her.

'Oh my God!' Emma jumped back, crashing to the floor and backpedalling until her back connected with the wall. 'Why would Amelia do that?'

Simran and Dylan had edged to the doorway upon seeing the macabre contents of the jar. The horror etched on their faces was mirrored by everyone in the room.

'We'll put your grandmother to rest,' Cara said. 'It's the least we can do.'

'She kept it as a trophy,' Kai snapped, covering the find with his jacket. 'Amelia is more dangerous than we anticipated, Cara. She's obsessed with Emma and not in a cute twin sister way.'

'I know,' Cara added, her voice strained, 'but we made the decision to stay here at Hartfield Manor. Now we have to defend it with our lives and keep everyone safe. Our mission hasn't changed. We will continue to recruit new vampires, and we will bring them into the Haven family. There are other Immortal families out there who are also a threat, but we can't let this derail our plans.' She waved in the direction of Flora's severed head in the jar.

Emma stood slowly, using the wall to steady herself.

'You must continue your work here, Cara. It's important that nobody feels alone and isolated out there in the world. We're all special, and we need to help each other more than ever before.'

'What are you going to do?' Simran asked, watching as Emma gathered the jar from the floor and cradled it to her chest.

'I'm going to hunt down Amelia and kill her for what she's done. I'm going to make her regret the day she ever woke her Dhampir sister.'

ACKNOWLEDGMENTS

Thank you, as always, to my children and parents who encourage and support me every step of the way. Massive thanks to my daughter for her expertise and assistance with TikTok!

A huge thank you to the publication team at BHC Press for all your hard work and support. Thanks to Stephanie, Hannah, Julia, and Sooz for helping me shape Emma's story into something special.

Finally, to my incredible readers who turn the pages of my books—without you, I wouldn't be able to do what I do. Thank you for your support and engagement.

ABOUT THE AUTHOR

Shelley Wilson is an English author of young adult fiction and adult self-help titles. She lives in the West Midlands, UK, with her three children and a mischievous black cat called Luna.

Her obsessions include anything mythical or supernatural, learning about Tudor and Viking history, exploring castles, and travelling in her VW Camper.